Sources *of* Light

Sources *of* Light

MARGARET McMULLAN

Houghton Mifflin
Houghton Mifflin Harcourt
Boston   New York   2010

Houghton Mifflin is an imprint of
Houghton Mifflin Harcourt Publishing Company.

www.hmhbooks.com

The text of this book is set in Weiss Medium.

Library of Congress Cataloging-in-Publication Data

McMullan, Margaret.
Sources of light / by Margaret McMullan.
p. cm.
Summary: Fourteen-year-old Samantha and her mother move to Jackson,
Mississippi, in 1962 after her father is killed in Vietnam, and during the
year they spend there Sam encounters both love and hate as she learns
about photography from a new friend of her mother's and witnesses
the prejudice and violence of the segregationists of the South.

ISBN 978-0-547-07659-1

[1. Coming of age—Fiction. 2. Race relations—Fiction. 3. Photography—
Fiction. 4. Segregation—Fiction. 5. Mississippi—History—
20th century—Fiction.] I. Title.
PZ7.M4787923So 2010
[Fic]—dc22
2009049708

Manufactured in the United States of America

DOC 10 9 8 7 6 5 4 3 2 1
4500214680

For Pat, who gives me courage always
and
For Jim Whitehead, who continues to inspire

CHAPTER 1

THE YEAR AFTER MY FATHER DIED, my mother took a job teaching at a small college in Jackson, Mississippi. It was 1962. I was fourteen years old. My father had been in the army, and when they came and told us about his death, they said that he stayed with his wounded soldiers after the helicopter crashed and that he died later under enemy fire. They said he was a hero, and I believed them.

The cicadas came that summer, the summer my mother and I moved to Jackson, and they made it nearly impossible to roller-skate, climb a tree, or generally do anything a person would want to do outside. With every step you'd hear *the*

Crunch. And even when you weren't stepping on their shells, you couldn't get away from the sound of them. Most days we could hear nothing but cicadas. Together they made a loud, sharp, nonstop noise that sounded like a hum and whistle combined, a sound my mother called "primordial." Even when I wasn't actually hearing them, I heard them in my mind. I imagined that I would be hearing that humming for years.

The morning of my first day of high school was no different. I was ready for the humming to stop. I was ready for the summer to be over. I was ready to fit in to this new town and make some friends.

To prepare me, my mother trimmed my bangs while I sat still on a stool at the bathroom sink. Over the summer I'd finally quit my bad habit of sucking on the ends of my hair. When my mother put down the scissors, I put on my cousin Tine's old green dress, snapped two plastic barrettes into my hair, ate a bowl of Frosted Flakes, then set out to walk the three blocks to school. Other girls at my school would be wearing new shoes and dresses. I knew this. My mother didn't think of things like new school clothes, though she always made sure I had books, pencils, and paper. Already we'd gone to her office at the college, where she'd opened the supply cabinet so that I could make my selections.

Jackson High School had been built next to the Baptist church, which had new swing sets, but we were supposed to be too old now to play on swings. Inside the school, the tile walls were the light green color of a public restroom, and the lobby display cases were full of football and cheerleading trophies, pretty much the only two extracurricular activities anyone bothered with.

This school was big, and there weren't many windows. There were a lot of corners and walls, and the hallways smelled of Bazooka bubblegum. I walked into my classroom and took a seat near the front.

I just sat there and mostly listened while everyone around me talked. They talked about Red Skelton's crazy costumes on last week's show, who was coming up next on *Ed Sullivan*, and which girls in our class already had hair in their armpits. The girls whispered about how a girl named Mary Alice McLemore had changed altogether over the summer. One girl whispered that Mary Alice wasn't chubby anymore, and couldn't they all see a training bra through her dress? She didn't even try to hide the outlines the straps made!

I didn't need a training bra. I hadn't grown much at all over the summer, up or out. My mother said I shouldn't be in such a hurry for my growth spurt, but I was still impatient for it.

When I finally figured out who Mary Alice was, I saw she wore a pink dress with a matching sweater. I didn't even know that girls' dresses came with matching sweaters. She wore pink knee socks too, the ribbed kind. She wore gold posts in her pierced ears. My mother wore earrings that clipped or screwed on. My mother promised me that someday soon I would get to wear clip-on pearl earrings.

Sometimes I thought the more money you had, the more you mattered. Who knows where I picked up that idea. Pittsburgh, where we used to live, maybe? Or maybe money was in the air that year in Jackson, like the buzz of those cicadas. My mother and I weren't rich, but we weren't poor either. There was my dad's army pension, and that summer we had collected enough S&H Green Stamps to redeem for an oscillating fan. We didn't buy anything my mother called "extra." We used dishes that came free in detergent boxes. My father did come from a good Mississippi family, whatever that meant. My mother was from Virginia. My parents had been young and good-looking when they met and married there, rich only in love. We'd gone to church when my dad was alive and now we didn't go to church.

In class, someone said something about the governor of Mississippi, Ross Barnett. Someone else said something about that man named Nixon who'd lost the presidential election two years before. Our teacher walked in and interrupted us: "Richard Nixon has snake eyes. People don't favor anybody with snake eyes, so now we have a Catholic in the White House."

Once again, even though I had spent the summer hoping,

I still hadn't gotten one of the *young* teachers, one of the *cool* teachers. I never did, no matter where we lived. Miss Jenkins was old and skinny, with peach fuzz hairs on her upper lip and all along her cheeks. She took attendance, and when she got to my name, she called me Samantha.

"People call me Sam," I said. I heard some giggling. Some boy said they had a dog named Sam. Miss Jenkins looked at me over her bifocals. She had a tiny pink nose, a nasally, country accent, and she kept a Kleenex tucked into her sleeve.

"All right then," she said. "Sam." She hissed it out, snake-like.

That first day and every day afterward Miss Jenkins wore a dark blue dress and stockings that sagged, the seams in the back going crooked by noon. She kept her salt-and-pepper-colored hair tied up in a bun, and we never saw her smile. She had two warped Ping-Pong paddles hanging by a leather hoop behind her desk. One had holes in it, one didn't. If we were lucky, we would get the one without the holes. That one would hurt less. We were in high school. We had grown out of playground equipment but we had not grown out of paddlings.

Miss Jenkins passed out our books and I opened one to the newer pages in the back, the only parts that hadn't been read by last year's class, and pressed my nose into the crease. These pages still had a new-book smell.

Miss Jenkins told us we had two big projects this school year. We would have to write a speech and we would have to speak it out loud to the class by the end of the year for a new subject called communications. She also gave us a used textbook called *Your Mississippi*, which she said we would need for our state report, part of which was due by Christmas. We were each supposed to do a report on Mississippi.

In science, we would get to use microscopes, beakers, and even Bunsen burners for our experiments, and I heard Mary Alice say it was no big deal because she had already done the same using her older brother's chemistry set.

When a boy came in late, Miss Jenkins sat him next to me. I didn't care. Boys didn't bother with me and I didn't bother with them, mostly because they had nothing to say. Most of them just spent all their time watching *Gunsmoke* or *Bonanza*.

He had black hair and his skin was powdery brown. I heard someone whisper that his father was full-blooded Choctaw. In Pittsburgh, I had known a boy who looked kind of like this boy, except that the boy I knew was called "colored." The boy I knew in Pittsburgh was named Alec. Once on a field trip our class took a bus to a factory outside of town to see how bread was made. We each got a free loaf. On the trip back, most of the kids tossed around their free bread loaves. Some even opened their bread on the bus, rolling the slices into dough balls and then using them as weapons, throwing them at one another or out the window at passing cars. We didn't say anything to each other, but Alec and I stayed close together in the back of the bus that day, tucking our loaves under our arms, keeping our free food safe. Neither of us dressed well, because our families didn't have much money. We were the same. After that day, Alec was my friend. He was my first friend, and I forgot that we were different colors. When I brought him over, my mother said how proud she was that I had a friend like Alec, that deep down, we were all the same. I thought she said that because he was a boy.

"I'm not too good with Indian names," Miss Jenkins said.

"Some folks call me Ears on account I have big ones," the boy said.

"All right then: Ears it is," Miss Jenkins said.

Miss Jenkins also announced that we would be having a dance at the school in November and our parents were welcome to be chaperones. I swallowed hard. I had never been to a dance—not here, and not at any of my other schools.

At lunch Ears asked me to sit with him, but I turned him down. I got brave and sat down at Mary Alice's table. The tanned girls went quiet as I opened my lunch: a peanut butter and banana sandwich wrapped in wax paper, which my mother still called parchment paper. For years I thought prisoners made the paper, because the name of the state prison in the Mississippi delta was Parchman. This is what I thought of each and every time I unwrapped my sandwich at lunch: prison.

Luckily, Mary Alice kept talking. She had spent her summer swimming and writing to the stars. Already she told us all she had received "correspondence" from Bobby Vinton, Connie Francis, and Brenda Lee. Then she turned to me. "Your name is Sam, right? So what did you do this summer?" Her pigtails were tied with pink grosgrain ribbon to match her pink dress and socks. I couldn't stop looking at all that pink.

"I got four jars just full up with cicada shells," I finally said. I didn't want to tell her anything about Pittsburgh or my dad or my mom crying all the time or our move. That was mine.

Mary Alice looked at me. I could follow her eyes moving from my home-cut bangs down to my green hand-me-down dress.

"That's what boys do," she said. "Collect bugs."

"Well," I started. It came out a whisper. "I collect the skeletons."

Mary Alice and her tanned friends laughed, and I laughed along with them as though I had meant what I said to be a joke.

Mary Alice and her friends seemed headed for what every other pretty girl in Mississippi was headed for: a beauty pageant. I was never going to be as pretty as Mary Ann Mobley or any of the other former Miss Mississippis, especially not in my cousin Tine's old stained dresses. My barrettes dug into my scalp and hurt my head all the rest of that day.

But then, in the afternoon, I saw him in the hallway as soon as the bell rang to let us out. He was tall and trim and he had a strong *man's* neck, not a boy's neck at all. He looked as though he would have a beard soon too, maybe even as soon as that fall. He smiled and waved to everyone as he walked, and when he saw me, he said, "Do I know you?" He had brown eyes shaded with dark brows, and his black hair was combed straight back.

"I'm Sam. I think someone in my class has a dog named Sam. Maybe you're confusing me with him." I stopped then. What had I done? I had just equated myself with a dog.

He laughed and shook his head. Then he did what any sensible boy would do: he walked past me and right on up to another girl, a prettier girl, Mary Alice McLemore, and my heart just sank. He leaned over her, and carried her books. They smiled and then walked out of the school together. Of course they went together. Of course. Mary Alice McLemore would never say anything as idiotic as what I had just said.

I picked up my blue canvas schoolbook satchel, another hand-me-down from my cousin Tine, and I started walking. As I headed home, I thought of my cousin. Tine was short for Clementine. She was one year older than I was, but she pulled weeds slower and had a tough time following my grandmother's instructions in the kitchen. Tine had what

9

they called a speech impediment. She stuttered and when she got scared, she drooled. The collars of Tine's shirts and dresses were always damp. I wore everything Tine wore. Would I end up stuttering, drooling and scared like Tine?

Outside, the air smelled clean, piney, and mildewy too. It used to be that by the end of most summers my feet were tough from going barefoot, and it made me happy and triumphant to know I could walk on hot, newly tarred streets, or even the tops of acorns when fall came. When school started, my feet were always strong going in. Not this year. All summer, I'd worn shoes because of the cicadas. My feet were soft. Maybe *I* wasn't tough enough for this new high school. Maybe I wasn't ready for this new year in our new hometown.

CHAPTER 2

I HAD BEEN AN ARMY BRAT and already I had lived in four other places: Virginia, North Carolina, Florida, and Pittsburgh, Pennsylvania. Pittsburgh was where we last saw my dad going off to a war in a country that most people hadn't even heard about yet: Vietnam. After Pittsburgh, my mother and I moved here to Mississippi near my father's hometown to start our new life together. My mother was an only child and both her parents had died even before I was born. This time, my mother said we were here to stay. She was hoping to turn her one-year contract into a lifetime job of teaching. My grandparents were about an hour outside of Jackson, in Franklin, where my father grew up. I knew a lot about Mississippi, or at least I thought I did, because while my mother finished her graduate schoolwork, I had spent every summer since I was born in Franklin with my grandparents. They lived near other relatives out in the country, where they kept a neat kitchen garden, which my cousin Tine and I helped to tend and harvest. Every July we worked with my grandmother to cook and can vegetables and fruit.

In Jackson, my mother and I lived on a quiet, shady street in a new subdivision that was still getting built. My grandfather told us that back in the 1940s, archaeologists had excavated what was part of a trench where the Chickasaw fought the Choctaw during the colonial Indian wars. But that didn't stop anybody from building houses there in 1962. Streets, houses, and yards now covered the area where Chickasaw and Choctaw once died. Sometimes I wondered if murder was in the soil.

Longleaf pines grew straight and tall like a giant's legs, dwarfing all the new houses. Most of the houses were like ours, ranch homes with open carports and big backyards. Tall pine trees hid the really ugly houses, and everywhere there were lines of monkey grass dividing lawns and properties. A line of monkey grass led you right up to our front door. We'd planted two sasanqua bushes, my father's favorite, at the corner of the house under my bedroom window. An old magnolia tree stood front and center in the backyard.

So far, I did not get along with the other girls my age on our street, the ones who played with Barbies and still mooned over Rhett Butler in *Gone With the Wind*. They all had bigger families, with mothers who stayed home and living fathers who sold lumber or cars.

My mother wasn't like their mothers and I wasn't like them. The inside of our house didn't even look like the insides of theirs.

As soon as we moved in, my mother painted our kitchen floor black and used the pages of cooking magazines to wallpaper the kitchen walls, painting over them with something glossy to seal them. But the paper puckered and the seal didn't quite work. Throughout the house was a black and brown carpet with a modern design that looked something like a bamboo forest, and all the walls were white, like the ones you see in museums.

When I got home from my first day of school, I took a sleeve of saltines out of the box on the counter and an open bottle of Coca-Cola from the refrigerator.

I sat with Willa Mae while she ironed. My mother didn't have snacks like Moon Pies or Little Debbies in the house. My mother told people she didn't "believe" in snacks, and I supposed it was the same belief system that prevented me from getting pierced ears. I knew we couldn't afford either.

"Why you like that old soda?"

"The flavor is enhanced and it doesn't hurt as much when you burp."

Willa Mae shook her head. "You a strange thing."

When Willa Mae ironed she kept an old Coca-Cola bottle filled with water near her. Every now and then, she put her thumb over the bottle and drizzled the water on the clothes to make for smoother ironing. My mother was the only mother I knew who wouldn't let her maid take our dirty clothes home with her. My mother thought that when Willa Mae left our house, she left her work behind, just like any other job.

Willa Mae owned her own house, and I heard her husband, who was a full-blooded Cherokee, left for a month, and then when he came back drunk she shot him, not dead, but wounded. And even though Willa Mae shot him, he still wanted to come back to her. They had a son I once met sitting in front of their swept yard, drawing pictures in the dust with a stick.

People who were really close to Willa Mae called her Bill. I wasn't close to Willa Mae, not the way other girls I knew said they were close to their maids, not the way I'd read about in all those old-timey novels about the South, not the way I thought I should be close. Early on when we moved into this house, my grandmother declared that if my mother was going to teach every day, someone had to be home when I came home from school, so she arranged for Willa Mae to come to our house every afternoon around three to clean, iron, and sometimes cook for an hour or until my mother came home. I figured that because Willa Mae knew someone else was paying her, she had decided not to allow herself to get too close to us. I guess she figured, who knew how long this arrangement would last?

I pressed my chin to my chest to check for any new developments. "Do you think I should be wearing a bra?"

Willa Mae glanced over my way briefly. She was as black as a person could be, and the white of her teeth glowed when she snickered. "That's not something you need."

My mother would be home soon. After teaching all day, she came home tired and took a thirty-minute nap. Sometimes she stayed there in her room, and I could hear her walking the floor. I knew she was thinking of my father then. I don't know how I knew, but I knew.

We heard two car doors slam shut in the carport. My mother came in through the back door, her arms loaded with papers and books. She was with a man.

He wore black jeans and pointy black boots and he was carrying a big canvas satchel and two bags of groceries. He had at least three cameras around his neck.

"Set the table, sweetie," my mother called in a singsong

voice. Her eyes crinkled shut when she laughed. "We've got company for dinner."

My mother introduced this man to me and to Willa Mae, who didn't look up but only nodded and continued ironing one of my mother's white shirts. His name was Perry Walker and he called me "kiddo" right off the bat. My mother suggested we all get started on dinner.

"I don't cook," I said, looking this Perry up and down. He laughed.

"She cooks all the time," my mother said, unpacking the groceries.

She set a pan of water on to boil and asked me to get the skillet.

"Do you teach with my mother?" My mother was already chopping an onion. I could hear Willa Mae in the next room, unplugging the iron, wrapping the cord around it. When Willa Mae had finished ironing, the shirts and everything else in the house smelled starchy and white. My mother and this Perry were messing up this good clean smell with their cooking. That night was supposed to be grilled cheese night for my mother and me, and it was supposed to be just us two.

"Perry just joined the faculty," my mother told me. "He moved from New York City in, what, July? Can you imagine how crazy this place must be to Perry, Sam? What do you think of this heat, Perry?"

"Are we talking weather or politics?"

"Oh, come on," my mother said. "It's not that bad."

"Depends on your definition of *bad*."

Perry told me he was a photographer and he was teaching a new class in photography.

"What kind of pictures do you take?"

"Everything. Wrecks, people, houses, you name it. But I draw the line at tree bark. I just don't want to see any more close-ups of tree bark." He laughed, carefully putting all the cameras hanging around his neck into his big satchel.

I stared at him. I couldn't help myself. What was this man doing in our kitchen, in our house?

"Perry's pictures have appeared in *Life* magazine, Sam," my mother said. "He's very talented."

Perry smiled and shrugged. "Anybody can take a good picture. I just happened to be around during catastrophic events. I guess that makes me an ambulance chaser."

"So what brings you here?" I asked.

He could have made a joke. He could have just said *teaching*. He could have made up something, but no. He went on as though I really cared because I was dumb enough to ask. He said he thought the South was this really amazing part of the country. He said that he sometimes went across town, across the tracks, into the houses of Negroes and took pictures of them and how they lived. He said that he believed that maybe, if people in the North and in the South saw them as people, eating cereal, doing laundry and folding clothes, sweeping their porches, just like everybody else does—if people knew their stories, maybe, just maybe, they'd quit lynching them.

"I'm ready, miss." Willa Mae stood at the kitchen's threshold holding her handbag, her hat already on. She wore shoes with the top tips cut out to give her toes room. We all grew quiet, knowing Willa Mae had heard that word *lynching*. Had this idiot Perry Walker forgotten she was only in the next room?

I just stood there and shook my head, hoping this Perry felt like the fool I thought he was. My mother taught me without ever having to tell me that you didn't discuss the race situation out loud. You just did the right thing, always. *We're all people*, she told me. *Black or white.* That's what her family believed and that's what my dad's family believed.

It never took my mother long to drive Willa Mae home because she lived only a few blocks away, but it was understood that Willa Mae would never walk home.

"I'll come with," I said, getting ready to leave. I could see Willa Mae smirk. She knew I'd much rather sit in the back seat with her. She could tell I didn't like this guy, Perry.

"No, you will not," my mother said. "You can help Perry with the rest of dinner."

When my mother left the house, she left behind a trail of sweet perfume.

"So. Are you one of those outside agitators?" My mother was gone now. I could say anything.

Perry laughed. "I'm just a photographer. The only thing I agitate is my camera and myself. Maybe some other teachers. And some students. Geez. I guess I'm an agitator." He opened a cabinet, saying he needed salt and pepper. Jars of peach, pear, fig, and plum preserves stood in a straight row before him like an army of Confederate soldiers, their masking tape labels made out in my grandmother's neat script. Perry stopped working on dinner and went to his big satchel, opened it, pulled out a camera, and this I couldn't believe. He started snapping pictures of my grandmother's preserves.

"My mother doesn't like photography. She prefers paintings." We had two paintings, one big enough to cover the wall behind the living room sofa. We called it the Spider because that was what it looked like most. Another painting hung in my mother's bedroom. It was a painting a student of hers had done of a medieval scene, but all the figures were out of proportion to the building they were in. I was never sure if that was on purpose.

Perry just smiled. He took some pictures of me sitting on the kitchen stool, even though I said I didn't like having my picture taken.

When my mother came back, I caught her fixing her hair and checking her reflection in the oven door.

Over spaghetti and garlic bread, my mother and this Perry Walker talked about their day and other faculty members. He did funny imitations of people, making my mother, and once even me, laugh. Then he started talking about things like contact sheets, cropping, and sepia toners.

"Why do you think you like taking pictures so much, Perry?" my mother asked. She turned up her hearing aid. She'd had polio as a child and lost most of her hearing in her right ear, but this was the first time in ages I'd seen her turn her aid up. Ever since the man from the military had come to our door to deliver the news about my father's death, she mostly turned her hearing aid down or off altogether. She put her elbow on the table, her face in her hand, and leaned in to listen. Crumbs stuck to her lipstick.

Perry shrugged. "Photography lets me get out of my own skin. I mostly bore myself."

Perry and I could both tell my mother was disappointed. She wanted an artsy answer. She wanted Perry to say something like *My pictures are a record of what the camera sees, not always what I see.* My mother was a sucker for art talk.

"Perry and I are going to give a series of art lectures at Tougaloo," my mother said. She knew I was getting bored. Tougaloo was an all-black college in Jackson. My mother's college was all white. Blacks weren't allowed to attend any college event. My mother told me only weeks before that the administrators at her college also discouraged faculty from teaching, visiting, or speaking at Tougaloo.

"Won't you get in trouble?" I asked.

My mother said she didn't care. They were wrong to impose such a ridiculous rule as keeping black people out of a public lecture at an institute for higher learning. Those were her words. She told me Perry was involved in the civil rights movement. "Last year I didn't know what to do about it." She looked at Perry then. "Now I do. If those students can't come to me, I'll go to them."

Perry smiled and raised his glass. They clinked glasses and drank to some silent toast. Had he put her up to this?

"You had your first day of school today too, right?" he said. "How was it? Have any big assignments to look forward to?"

I had to admit I liked that he said this and not *How was your day?* Or *Did you make any nice new friends?* He asked me in a way that made me feel older, like we were working together.

"There's going to be a dance in November," I said. "Miss Jenkins needs chaperones."

"That's one parent duty I could sign up for," my mother said. "I'll call her in the morning."

Then I told them about my state project. Perry said he remembered those kinds of assignments. "Please, please don't be one of those kids who cut out pictures from a magazine, then glue them into a collage on posterboard."

That was exactly what I had planned on doing.

"Okay. So what should I do?"

"Easy. Take your own pictures."

"I don't have a camera."

"Here." He gave me the camera he had been using. "Now you do. Take it. Really. It's an old one, but reliable."

My mother went through all the reasons Perry shouldn't and couldn't lend me his old camera, but he insisted. "This camera is like me. It's indestructible. Really. Tell you what. Try it out, and if you like it, well, we'll see how it goes. Deal?"

It was a black Asahi Pentax, and it was heavy. He showed me how to load film and batteries and how to use the one lens.

"Film is cheap," he said. "Use it."

He showed me how to focus and refocus, telling me that exposure was based on the quantity of light that reached the film. Overexposure made negatives too dark, while under-exposure made negatives too light.

When he tried to explain about the light and the shutter and how the aperture or lens opening could be adjusted like the iris of your eyes, I told him to stop because I didn't get it.

"All you have to know now is that a camera is like your eye. To focus, keep one eye closed, while you're looking with the other. It brings everything closer," he said. "You can hide behind a camera."

This I got. This I liked.

"What should I take pictures of?"

He said the word *photography* came from two Greek words that meant "light drawing." Drawing with light. "I know," he said, looking at the expression on my face. "I sound like a pinhead, don't I? But this stuff is cool. Light makes photography possible. Photographers have their own reality. Sometimes the ideas are more important than the subject. We can be like painters. Maybe even better."

"So?" I said. I hated when grownups didn't just answer a question. "What should I take pictures of?"

He looked at me. "Anything you would paint. Anything you look at or wonder about or want to know more about." He closed the camera, wound the film, then lifted it to his right eye and snapped a picture of my mother.

For dessert, we had some of the jarred peaches Tine and I canned with my grandmother, and I took a few pictures of my mother and Perry eating them.

At school, instead of having gym class, we made white roses out of Kleenex, tying them with green pipe cleaners for parent-teacher night. Then, the following night, on parent-teacher night, Mary Alice made fun of Miss Jenkins outside in the hall while her little brother, Jeffy, made off with half the cookies. Through the closed door, I could hear Mary Alice's mother paying Miss Jenkins compliments, making up nice things Mary Alice had never said about her.

When her turn came that night, my mother just crossed her legs and listened. I overheard Miss Jenkins tell my mother how sorry she was to hear about my father, how highly she regarded him, how it seemed too that I was having a tough time making friends. It turned out that Miss Jenkins knew my father from way back in Franklin, back when he was in high school and she was starting out in her teaching career. That's how old Miss Jenkins was. Then I overheard my mother tell Miss Jenkins that she wasn't much of a cookies-and-milk mom, but she was very good when it came to course work. *Course work.* Those were her words. That and *curriculum.* I couldn't see the expression on Miss Jenkins's face, but I could only imagine. Did Kleenex roses count as course work? I think I even heard my mother tell Miss Jenkins that she believed that an ordinary life wasn't good enough, that it was supposed to be special.

My mother left parent-teacher night without eating one cookie, whispering to me, "I see we're going to have to supplement."

Two weeks later, Miss Jenkins told us it was time we all started thinking seriously about our state reports. She didn't tell us exactly how we should do this. I considered my options, thinking mostly about the camera Perry had loaned me and loaded for me. What *did* I wonder about?

I usually got up early most mornings, but now I went out with a camera. There was something about walking around up and down the street in our subdivision while everyone else was asleep—something secretive and special. Some mornings, it felt as though I were still dreaming, and I snapped fuzzy close-ups of bugs, bird's nests, rocks, a patch of lawn, or my own dewy, grass-covered feet.

One morning, I climbed on top of a cinder block to get to the high shelf in our carport where my mother kept my dad's old army coat and his scratchy moss green army blanket. He had used these in Korea, and when he came back, he said he really didn't want to give them away but he didn't want to look at them either. After he died, my mother felt the same— she couldn't give them away, but she couldn't look at them either. I spread the coat out on the carport cement, bending the right sleeve in a salute. I took its picture.

In science we read about monkeys and someone in class asked if it was really possible that we came from monkeys. Miss Jenkins listened and nodded, then told us not to think too hard on such things.

I wondered about people. I thought about Willa Mae's days. When I sat and talked with her she was at the kitchen sink or standing over the ironing board. I thought about how much of her time, how much of her day was spent staring into a kitchen sink. I took a picture of the kitchen sink, just as she left it, the soap bubbles still there, popping. I climbed up on a stool and took a picture of her dark, dry hands smoothing the wrinkles flat over my mother's pleated gray teaching skirt. I took a picture of her pinning our sheets on the clothesline, then of her throwing them up like parachutes as she made our beds. She didn't smile for the camera. She wasn't like that. But we laughed some.

At school, after a month had passed, we all came to realize that Mary Alice had a pair of knee socks to match every different colored skirt she owned. And most days she told the class of new ways her little brother, Jeffy, pulled a practical joke on their maid. He especially enjoyed spraying shaving cream into his pillowcase on sheet-changing day.

Next in science we began to study the earth, the solar system, and the other planets. In the classroom, Miss Jenkins used new satellite photos, and it all looked so different from the way it had in seventh or eighth grade. Less perfect. Our moon was pockmarked with craters. There weren't any of the black lines that divided our states or made up our country's borders as we'd learned from our one-dimensional maps.

Perry was coming over all the time now. He taught me how to develop my pictures. He had two darkrooms, one at his home and one at the college. We used the one at the college because he said it was big enough for the two of us. His processing trays were lined up in a neat row. Holding his print tongs, he showed me how to wash and dry prints. He taught me how to make contact sheets and proof sheets. He told me about resin-coated prints, resolutions, and photo composites. While he talked about different exposures and their effects, he showed me how to mix the chemicals, how to soak, wash, and then dry the paper.

"It's magic, isn't it?" he said.

Seeing the pictures appear, the images coming out of the blank paper soaking in the neat rows of trays filled with clear liquid, went beyond magic.

The first pictures we developed were the pictures I'd taken of things I wondered about: my dad's army coat, the kitchen sink after Willa Mae had been there.

"Your mom told me about your dad," Perry said, looking at the picture of the coat. "I bet you miss him."

I didn't say anything. I couldn't. It didn't feel right telling this man about my dad. My throat choked at the thought. He'd always held my hand when I was scared, even when I shouldn't have been. He read to me at night. He could cook and hunt and farm and do just about anything. His helicopter crashed. He stayed with his men. And now? Now I was beginning to forget what he smelled like.

CHAPTER 3

AT SCHOOL MISS JENKINS TALKED ON AND ON about The War, which was The War Between the States, which was The Civil War, which I thought I'd left behind in middle school. It seemed as though everyone in my class had great-grandfathers or great-uncles who either fought or survived during Civil War times. Everybody took turns telling her own version about what happened at the battle of Chancellorsville or at Brice's Cross-roads.

"So you see, the Civil War wasn't only about slavery at all," Miss Jenkins finally said, looking over the top rim of her glasses, daring us. We were nearing the end of the section. "It was about states' rights."

"The South should have won," Jimmy Ray said. "We had more reason to win. We just ran out of food and money. The North sure didn't win because they were better'n us, that's for sure."

People in my class who usually didn't say anything were talking. They were saying things that sounded a lot like what their parents probably told them. People had done this at my old school in Pittsburgh last year too.

"Many scholars have written a great deal on this very subject," Miss Jenkins said.

Mary Alice raised her hand. She said her mother was in the Junior League and was applying for membership to the Daughters of the American Revolution. "My family is very involved in states' rights."

Miss Jenkins smiled. "Sam, your mother teaches college. What does she have to say about the reasons the South lost the war?" I could tell Miss Jenkins was used to judging her students quickly, and that she had marked me as a no-good, and too big for my britches. I wasn't cute enough for her to like either.

"My mom teaches art history," I said. Everyone was looking at me and I wanted to run and hide. "She's never said anything about the war." And that was true. She told me about the Spanish Civil War, and how that violence affected what Picasso and Miro painted, but nothing about the American Civil War. My mother tended to be more interested in what was happening outside of Mississippi.

That afternoon my mother and I were standing in the frozen food aisle of the Jitney when I saw Mary Alice with her mother. They had on matching outfits—blue shorts suits with red gingham piping with red front pockets and red sandals. Mary Alice was holding her pink ballet shoes. My mother couldn't afford the ballet lessons that Mary Alice and her friends attended across town.

I was still wearing last summer's shorts, which fit too tightly. I checked to make sure that my top still covered the waistband, which I had safety-pinned closed.

Our mothers introduced themselves. Mary Alice's mother said she knew we were new in town, that she'd heard about my father and all and she was real sorry about what happened.

"You're very kind," my mother said, all serious, touching her arm. "Thank you."

"Can you believe how fast they grow up nowadays?" Mary Alice's mother said, anxious to change the subject, looking at Mary Alice and me as though we weren't listening.

My mother smiled and nodded.

"Regular little ladies."

"Sam still likes roller skating and climbing trees though."

At least she didn't say *and playing with her dolls* too.

"So I bet you're looking forward to Mary Alice's birthday party tonight," Mary Alice's mother asked me. I caught the look Mary Alice gave her mother, but I didn't say anything.

"You remember," Mary Alice said. "I told you about it at school. It's tonight. The slumber party? You remember. You're supposed to come dressed as your mother." Mary Alice looked my mother and me both up and down. I could smell her dislike for us the same way I could smell the air right before it rained. "But you might have forgotten and already made other plans." She said this hopefully.

"Oh, Sam doesn't have any plans," my mother said. "This will be hilarious, Sam. You can go dressed like me. What a riot!" Nobody said *hilarious* or *riot*. My mother picked up new ways of saying things from her students. Her enthusiasm embarrassed me. Why couldn't she just talk like everyone else? Sometimes I thought she tried her hardest *not* to sound like everybody else.

I could feel Mary Alice and her mother staring at us. They looked so perfect in their matching clothes. At least my mother wasn't wearing her dungarees. Unlike in Pittsburgh, women didn't wear pants in Mississippi—only pedal pushers with gingham cuffs matched with gingham shirts. But ever since my father died, my mother took to wearing dungarees, my father's old loose shirts, and flat shoes after work and on the weekends.

"Well, good," Mary Alice's mother said to my mother. "Maybe you can go kick up your heels while Sam's with us. I know some wonderful bachelors if you're ever up for a blind date."

"They'd have to be really blind," my mother said, attempting a joke. "In both eyes."

At home, while my mother sat at her desk, typing, I looked through her closet for an outfit to wear to Mary Alice's dress-like-your-mom slumber party. My mother bought only teaching clothes—cardigan sweater sets and A-line skirts with kick pleats in the back. My mother's closet held five of these skirts in various shades of gray, three dresses, one dark blue, one gray, one black, three pairs of shoes, my dad's old work shirts, his army uniform, and the perfectly folded flag the army had given my mother. After the legionnaires fired the shots at my dad's military funeral, they presented my mother with the flag and the gun shells too, telling her that her husband had not died in vain. I wondered if that helped.

He had joined the army in Mississippi, then he was stationed in Virginia, where he met my mother. After they married and when I was two, he was shipped off to Korea. He came back a lieutenant. I was four. For years, it was just the three of us moving around from state to state. We were happy. In North Carolina we camped in the mountains. When we lived in Florida we went to the beach when we could. When I was nine, we moved to Pittsburgh, and it was perfect. We visited the libraries and museums at Carnegie Mellon and we took long walks along the Ohio, the Allegheny, and Monongahela rivers, all of us together. My dad had a steady income, and my mother worked on her graduate degree in art history. That was before he left for Vietnam. Then when his helicopter went down, it was as if *we* went down too. Boom. Simple as that—the happy *we* of our family was over.

My mother kept the stack of letters from his war years and my dad's Purple Heart medal on the top shelf, even though everybody said she should have the medal mounted, framed, and hanging in some main room of our house. She kept my dad's army picture there on that top shelf too. It was framed in wood. In it he's almost too handsome, with his dark flattop, his Elvis half-smile, his ears sticking out from his army beret making him more real and more like a dad. I knew him only for a little while really, given his whole lifetime. I remember when he and my mom swung me between them on the beach we liked visiting when we lived in Tallahassee. We caught crabs there to boil and eat at night. My mother put the water on and my father and I put in the crabs. He taught me how to eat them. He taught me about other things too: helping out around the house, respecting my grandparents, being nice to my cousin Tine, helping others fit in. The summer before he left for the last time, we were cracking and eating crabs when he talked to me about honor and respect, duty and discipline. He told me I should always do what I said I was going to do and that I should always do the right thing.

"How am I supposed to know what the right thing to do is?" I asked.

He shrugged and smiled, then put his hand on my head, his fingers stretching across. "You'll just know."

I ran my hand across the top shelf of my mother's closet and caught ahold of the bundle of old letters tied with blue ribbon—letters written by my mother addressed to my dad while he was overseas. My mother and I didn't talk about my dad much, or the exact details of how he died. I couldn't even say any of the words like *passed away* or *dead*. I thought to say those words would make it really so; so not to say them could mean that he was still alive.

"I don't remember—did he ever write back?" I held the letters out for my mother to see and take.

"He did. They're in there too." She pushed her chair back, took the bundle, and thumbed through the pages. She reopened a few and showed me.

Inside the letters were locks of her hair, menus from restaurants, prayer cards, a page of poetry from a book.

"He used to love to read in bed every night, especially to

you. Remember? When I wrote him, I tried to keep things cheery."

"He put *Ha* here. And look, *Ugh*." I pointed out his handwriting in the margins of her letters.

"It was like having a conversation," she said, tying the letters back up with the ribbon. She must have seen my expression.

"You can have the picture," she said. "If you want."

Sometimes I imagined what it would have been like if my dad were still alive. I thought of us picking him up after work at the barracks, or maybe after the war he would have gotten out of army life altogether. He'd come home with a briefcase, his tie loosened and his suit jacket slung over one shoulder, his tired eyes hidden behind sunglasses maybe. When he was alive, he gave me these tight, close hugs each time before he left, and then again when he came home. I could always count on those two tight moments with him.

I went and put the framed picture of my dad on my nightstand, then came back to my mother's room.

"How's the dressing-up-like-me coming along?"

I held up one of her gray skirts.

"You'll need something on top."

My mother had drawers full of sweaters mostly dark blue, gray, and black. She owned one girdle, but she never wore it. When she thought to, my mother wore slips. As usual, my options were limited, to say the least.

"That reminds me," I said. I told my mother about the dance coming up at our high school, and even though no one had asked me to it yet, I asked her if I could please please please get a brassiere. I could feel my face turn red and hot when I said the word out loud. "All the other girls are wearing them."

She said she didn't see why I couldn't just wear a slip, but *okay, okay, okay.*

Meanwhile, my mother was telling me about some princess in Italy who was being taught to paint by Kokoschka. "Can you imagine?" my mother said. "I bet she has no idea how lucky she is."

I thought for a minute, then said, "Who's Kokoschka, and why do you even care?" I had just asked her for my first brassiere and she was talking about some painter with a weird name. Sometimes my mother's talk made my head hurt.

I put on the gray skirt and a white shirt, and bobby socks and loafers. I looked at myself in the mirror, shifting to a forward-tilting hunch I had seen a magazine model do. My mother and I were almost the same height, but even in grays she was more beautiful. I just looked like a boy. I pushed my hair away from my forehead. I took my ponytail out, then put it in again. It had looked better before I bothered with it. At least she let me wear lipstick to Mary Alice's party. And soon, soon I would have a bra.

Early that evening, Perry came over and set up his tripod outside, and he lit up all the rooms in the house even though he said he preferred daylight and didn't like using artificial lights. He wanted my mother to walk back and forth in the living room while he stood outside taking pictures. He said he was going for a kind of effect that would make my mother look like a ghost. It had something to do with the shutter in the camera being open longer that would make the walking blur. He was staying for dinner too. They were celebrating because one of his photographs had appeared in a book and someone had called him and asked if he could put together a whole collection of pictures for his own book.

My mother announced that this was the beginning of something.

Before my mother drove me, dressed as her, to the party, Perry insisted on taking my picture.

"Say gumbo," Perry said.

"Cheese," I said.

When I put my hands on my hips, he told me to quit posing. "We have enough grinning automatons in this world." He started snapping pictures. "And the people sat down to eat and drink, and rose up to play," he said, his eye still pressed in to his camera, his finger still snapping pictures. He kept his left eye closed. I rolled my eyes. This dude was crazy.

"What's that from?" my mother asked, standing near him. She was holding his drink.

"Exodus."

It made me feel weird knowing that my mother was going to be alone that night with Perry Walker. Usually it was the *three* of us. Why couldn't she just sit home by herself, eat some gingersnaps, look through her box of glass slides, and work on her lecture notes like she always did on Friday nights? When she wasn't teaching, my mother sat at her desk, typing on her big black Underwood typewriter. She wore my dad's old flannel work shirt and a pair of men's dungarees held up by an old belt buckled to the last hole. That's when she seemed most herself.

"Now the two of you together," Perry said, getting his camera ready.

My mother and I stood next to each other, my mother smiling, her arm around me, me staring straight ahead.

Already, Perry was telling my mother about his morning at the Petrified Forest. "I should take you and Sam there. Even if you've been, that place is amazing! Sam, have you *seen* that petrified log called the Caveman's Bench?" I nodded and rolled my eyes again. Everyone in Jackson knew about the Petrified Forest and the Caveman's Bench, which was really a huge stone log from prehistoric times. But before I could say anything, Perry was already talking about something else. There was a writer he'd met at the grocery store, an older woman named Eudora Welty. He wanted to invite her to speak at the college. "She started off taking pictures for the Work Projects Administration—you know, the WPA—back in the 1930s. Great pictures of people out in the country, working, dancing, or leaning on a front porch."

"People around here call her Miss Welty," my mother said. "I love her stories. Ed gave me a volume of them when we first met." My mother said my father's name so casually, so easily, it put a chill up my spine.

It was like both of them couldn't wait to get rid of me so they could talk on and on.

We all arrived at once. Ten girls and me. Mary Alice came to the door dressed up in a low-cut dress. She held an unlit cigarette in one hand and an empty wineglass in the other, and supposedly imitated her mother. "Darling, I really think this neckline sends a message, don't you?"

She walked all us girls around her house, which smelled of lemon-scented Pledge.

They lived in a split-level home, the only split-level home I had ever seen. Because of the stairs, the pool outside, the shag carpeting, and the television in their kitchen, I decided Mary Alice and her family were the wealthiest, most important people in Mississippi. Her father had something to do with furniture—sofas and bedroom suites, which Mary Alice called *suits*. She said her father traveled to Birmingham and Mobile a lot. All of their furniture matched.

We toured their concrete fallout shelter downstairs. The two-room area was separated and walled off from the laundry room and the rest of their downstairs. As all us girls came down the steps, we saw him, the handsome boy from school, cycling on a stationary bike in a T-shirt wet with his sweat. He smiled when all of us came in, and he lifted his hand in a casual wave, as if he were cycling through the backstreets of France or Italy. Some of the girls giggled. I stopped breathing. A TV was on with local news about another Negro church burning.

Mary Alice pointed out their new sectional sofa for when the Russians attacked. She showed us all the canned food they stored in there too: Sanka, Carnation instant dry milk, and a box of instant whipped potatoes, which nothing, not even a nuclear explosion, could get me to eat. But nobody much cared for Mary Alice's fallout shelter tour. We were too busy smiling at the only boy in the stuffy room.

He had fun in his brown eyes. I saw too that his ears stuck out. So he wasn't so handsome after all. That made me like him even more.

I wished I had my camera then, to take a picture and to hide behind. I'd keep one eye closed to focus, the way Perry said to do. To bring what you want to capture closer.

"That's her brother Stone," one of the girls told me, because, I supposed, everyone knew this but me.

Stone got off the bike and switched the TV channel to *The Twilight Zone*, where a man on a plane looked out the window and saw a gorilla monster messing with the plane's wing.

My breath came back. "Oh. I thought." But I stopped myself. Mary Alice McLemore did not need to know that I thought her brother was her boyfriend.

Nobody heard me anyway. It was obvious I was one big accidental invitation. Mary Alice was busy explaining to us how a family of five can live comfortably in their fallout shelter for two weeks until radiation decreased outside. Like some television host, she pointed toward the built-in cabinets with the map of the world and a map of Mississippi thumbtacked on.

Then she showed us to the powder room even though nobody needed to go. Mary Alice's mother had set up the powder room with a full supply of cosmetics and hairspray just for us.

I attempted to fit in to this craziness. These girls were carrying around empty white patent leather purses with gold clasps and wearing matching shoes and pillbox hats, all the things their mothers wore every day, or so I imagined. I was of course dressed as my mother, looking more like a coed and not a posh lady with pearls and kid gloves. Mary Alice's little brother, Jeffy, buzzed around us dressed as an astronaut in a silver space suit that zippered up the front, silver boots, and a big plastic bubble the size and shape of a fish tank over his head. Each time he circled around to me, he kicked my shin. Nobody said anything.

Mary Alice led us all upstairs and over to a silver tray set up with glasses and bottles on the dining room table. She offered us drinks, pouring cherry Kool-Aid from a rum bottle. We sat at the table eating fish sticks, potato chips, and Twinkies.

It came time for Mary Alice to open her birthday presents. While we all gathered round and watched, Mary Alice ripped open colorful packages of headband sets, a shorts outfit, a record player that lifted up like a little suitcase, a record holder for all her 45s, and most all the hits she didn't already have.

Mary Alice was fifteen, and I had gotten her exactly what I wanted, a sparkly Hula-Hoop. It was wrapped in the Sunday funnies. Whenever a present needed wrapping my mother had me use the funny papers because, she said, it was "artistic." I knew it was just plain cheap. When Mary Alice came to my gift, she hesitated, actually reading one of the comics and smiling.

"This is really funny," Mary Alice said, not laughing.

"So funny I forgot to laugh," I heard someone say.

Mary Alice put the Hula-Hoop aside. I thought I heard someone whisper something about my crazy mother and cheap kid toys.

Little Jeffy forgot he had the astronaut bubble on his head as he tried to eat a Twinkie. His face was pinched up into a little fist. I laughed at him. I knew it was mean of me to laugh at him, but he *had* kicked me, and I laughed even more when I saw that the inside of his fish tank bubble was getting nasty-looking with all his mouth slobber on the side.

Mary Alice laughed too, not at me, but at her own little brother. Then she said I was funny. I wasn't sure what to say to this. Someone said something about if you kissed your elbow, you'd turn into a boy.

"Who wants to practice kissing?" Mary Alice said.

They all squealed and ran toward Mary Alice's room. I followed. I had never been to Mary Alice's room. I had never kissed or practiced kissing. I was never so scared in all my life. Why couldn't we just tell ghost stories or braid one another's hair like we used to do at all the other birthday parties in all the other towns I'd ever lived in?

Mary Alice had all-white bedroom furniture—even her own desk with three drawers and a matching chair. Everything matched, with gold hardware. Her walls were a pink she called "blush," and she had a pink bedspread, a pink bed ruffle, a pink ruffled lampshade, and a pink canopy on her bed. I had always wanted a canopy bed.

By the time I finished looking around, somebody had turned out the lights and every girl was already kissing and hugging a pillow in the corners of the room. Luckily there were no pillows left. While the other girls giggled, Jeffy stomped and jumped in circles, pestering them. He burrowed between girls and pillows while Mary Alice screamed that he was acting like a pervert.

I excused myself to the powder room down the hall. On the way, I passed another bedroom, with walls almost completely covered with posters of rocket ships, and astronauts standing in front of their machinery at Cape Canaveral, and pictures of planets taped to the ceiling above the bed. There was a pile of clothes in the corner, and shoes everywhere. The bed wasn't made and the blankets and sheets were whipped up like one of my grandmother's meringues. A catcher's mitt sat on a wooden bureau alongside a watch laid smooth. A bookcase beside the bed held volumes of the *Encyclopedia Britannica*, something I had always wanted for myself.

"Come on in," Stone said, popping up from his chair.

Standing there at his door, I jumped, terrified and embarrassed that he had caught me spying.

The TV was on with news about NASA's Project Mercury. The announcer talked about aero systems, satellite orbits, thermal and atmospheric systems, and secondary power equipment. The announcer reminded us that in May of that year, Kennedy had vowed that the United States would get to the moon first. "Now is the time to take longer strides," Kennedy had said. It had been five years since *Sputnik* blasted off from the Soviet Union.

He had a TV in his room! Never mind lunar conquests. Stone McLemore had a TV in his room!

He had posters of what he called space hardware: one was a TIROS 1. I looked at what he showed me and named. I tried to see the beauty in the hydrogen tanks, circuitry, fuel cells, and docking lights.

"See this?" he said, pointing to a map of the moon. "This shows the eight suitable sites to land. The Sea of Tranquility is the ultimate target."

"Makes sense," I said. Maybe I even liked him because of his name. I had never known anyone called Stone before, and it made him special, worthy of something.

He showed me a poster from Union Carbide, where he said he wanted to work someday to help manufacture aircraft and guided missiles. He pointed out the small print: "For reasons of security, the missile shown here is an artist's conception— not a drawing of an existing weapon."

When I saw Stone's profile, when I saw the little slope of his nose and the pout of his lip, I wished then that I had Perry's Pentax to snap a picture for keeps.

"Is it possible that the planets swirling around the sun eventually just swirl into the sun, like a whirlpool?"

Stone laughed, then he looked at me, considering. "Cool."

The TV news shifted from cooling systems and rockets to violent demonstrations in Alabama.

"It's all a Communist plot, you know," Stone said, turning toward the TV. "And these news people are making us look like rednecks. We're just trying to protect our people and our states."

"I know," I said, not knowing what else to say.

"This is a war."

I thought about that little word *war* and all the bignesses it caused, like my dad's death. I couldn't understand why or how Stone would use that word. I couldn't even understand the word.

"You might not know that yet," he said.

I didn't know what he could mean. Wars were fought in other countries. My dad had fought in two wars. Korea and then Vietnam. We weren't in any war here though. We ate sugared cereal and drank milk. There weren't even any rationings. Who was the enemy? The black people who lived down the street? Willa Mae? A war, here in Mississippi? Mississippi hadn't been involved in a war since The War, which was The Civil War, but that was over, wasn't it?

"You need protecting," he said. "We got to protect the women of the South, girls like you. That's what my mom says."

I had to smile. How could I not? Hadn't the handsomest

boy I had ever talked to in my fourteen years of living on this earth just said that he was going to protect me?

We turned to watch the TV. The local anchorman was saying something about a boy named Virgil who'd been riding on the handlebars of his brother's bicycle when he was fatally shot by white teenagers.

"Oh, that's terrible," I said, putting my hand over my mouth, feeling sick at the news.

"It is." He got up and turned off the TV.

"Guess I'd better get back," I said.

Stone just nodded. He seemed distracted.

When I got back to Mary Alice's room, Jeffy had taken off his fish tank helmet and was whizzing around in his space suit.

"Get out of here," Mary Alice yelled at her little brother. Then she called him a name we never ever ever used. Not in our family ever, north or south. We said Negro or colored or black. The bad boys at school used that other word. But this girl, Mary Alice, she just said it, out loud, like that, like she said it every day. I had never heard a girl, no matter how old, speak this way, and it gave me a queer, cold, sick feeling.

"You're not the boss of me," Jeffy said, and stomped out of the room.

"I'm bored," one girl said, throwing down her pillow date, not caring what Mary Alice had just said.

"Let's keep on talking like grownups," another girl said, tossing her pillow alongside the other.

"Mary Alice?" I finally said. "Can we just go outside now?"

And all at once we were changing to swim in Mary Alice's swimming pool.

"Do my straps, will you?" Mary Alice asked me. Me! I was helping Mary Alice with her swimsuit. Her skin was a perfect brown and her sparrow shoulder blades jutted out like wings.

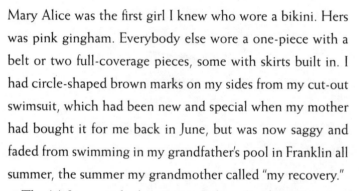

Mary Alice was the first girl I knew who wore a bikini. Hers was pink gingham. Everybody else wore a one-piece with a belt or two full-coverage pieces, some with skirts built in. I had circle-shaped brown marks on my sides from my cut-out swimsuit, which had been new and special when my mother had bought it for me back in June, but was now saggy and faded from swimming in my grandfather's pool in Franklin all summer, the summer my grandmother called "my recovery."

The McLemores had an in-ground pool *with* landscaping. We all took turns with the Hula-Hoop I had given Mary Alice. She said she had four others, but none with pink and silver sparkles like this one.

When Mary Alice's brother Stone brought out a tray of Coca-Colas, I jumped into the pool so he wouldn't see me in my suit. I didn't like the idea of being almost completely naked in front of anyone, let alone Stone. It wasn't that I was shy. It was mostly because I didn't think I looked too good almost naked.

Sneaking stares at him again, I decided he was surely the handsomest boy I had ever seen. This was a boy you want to marry. This was a boy who was good and kind because he said women needed protecting and he brought out Coca-Colas for his kid sister's birthday party.

Some of the girls played how-long-can-you-hold-your-breath, swimming underwater the length of the pool, some-times twice. Stone dived in, and he didn't make a big show of taking in his breath before he went under. After one length, two lengths, then half of the third length of the pool, he shot up from the deep end, laughing and gasping for air, his hair spraying a crown of thousands of water drops. Yes. He really was the most beautiful handsome boy I'd ever seen.

Paddling around in the deep end, I realized then and there that, excluding her kid brother, Jeffy, Mary Alice had the per-fect family and the perfect life. When you're an only child in a family with an only parent, you look at other, bigger fami-lies with envy. Mary Alice had a family with a station wagon, a split-level house, and a pool.

But then I looked up and saw Mary Alice's toes, as she stood at the edge of the diving board. Her second toe lay on top of her big toe on each foot. I had never seen such a thing. I wondered if Mary Alice's toes would ever prevent her from doing the things she wanted to do in life.

"Look, y'all!" she said, forming her perfect body into a perfect swan's dive. I decided then that any time I got frustrated with my overall situation in life, mad or jealous of knee socks or a pink canopy bed in a pink room, I'd take a deep breath and think about Mary Alice's toes. At least I didn't have Mary Alice's toes.

We swam until the sun set and then changed into our sleep clothes. Mary Alice wore a nightgown that my mother would have had me wear as a good party dress. Everybody else wore baby-doll pajamas with bloomer panties. I wore one of Tine's old faded cotton nightgowns.

That night Mary Alice showed us her most prized possession: a Doublemint chewing gum wrapper signed by Elvis, framed in a gold-colored frame. Mary Alice said that two summers ago her daddy heard that Elvis was back home in Tupelo and the McLemores had a cousin who lived there, and that McLemore cousin called over to the one hotel in town and said, "What room is Elvis staying in?" When the cousin went over to the hotel, there were two white Cadillacs parked out front with I LOVE YOU in red lipstick covering the cars. A real pretty blond woman came to the door and said, "Would you like an autograph?" All that McLemore cousin had was a gum wrapper. And when Elvis himself came to the door, he signed it. Elvis signed Mary Alice McLemore's cousin's Doublemint chewing gum wrapper, and that little gum wrapper is what got Mary Alice hooked on celebrity signatures.

"How do we know you're not making all that up?" one girl asked. "How do we know Elvis signed it and not you?"

"Because he did and I don't lie and you're just going to have to believe me."

I stared at Mary Alice then, watching her every move. I would never be one of those girls who screamed at the way Elvis moved when he sang, only because I was too shy, not because he didn't do me the same way. But if I had a chewing gum wrapper signed by Elvis Presley, I would have said a lot of other stuff to defend it. Mary Alice only said what she said, and you had to admire that.

We spent the rest of the night painting one another's fingernails, a luxury my mother had never allowed. I could hear the wind outside blowing and laughing, trying to tell me something, warn me maybe. I thought of the cicadas already buried deep in the soil, sleeping, maybe getting geared up to come out again in seven years. All the other girls were still so chatty on the floor in sleeping bags and pallets, which was good, because all I had to do was listen to their voices until I fell asleep while outside the last of the cicadas hummed.

CHAPTER 4

THE FOLLOWING MORNING at Mary Alice's house, we ate breakfast in a glassed-in patio the McLemores called their Florida breakfast room, because that's where they had breakfast. I couldn't imagine having a room just for one meal. We drank instant Tang, and they could even afford grapefruit juice in a can.

I thought of how Mrs. McLemore must have seen her life, as if she were in some TV commercial: *Mrs. Jack P. McLemore enjoys making breakfasts in their sunny Florida room.* "There are plenty of outlets and it's more relaxing here," she told us, as if she were addressing her fans. She fried up a mess of sausages and pancakes in an electric skillet on their glass coffee table. Still, it was nice that she went to so much trouble just for us girls. I'd never seen a mother do so much for her daughter.

Mary Alice's father and Stone took their breakfasts in the kitchen because, I guessed, they didn't want to eat with all us girls. I peeked in at them while they were both reading the morning paper, talking to each other in low, serious voices about world events. Mr. McLemore looked up and said good morning. Then out of nowhere, he said, "I understand your mama is a school person and your daddy was a war hero. He was from a fine family, your daddy was." The way Mr. McLemore said this made me both proud and uncomfortable. For some reason he singled me out and I didn't like being singled out for anything.

"We always have pancakes on Saturdays," Mary Alice told us girls back at the table. She said she also got to watch *Lawrence Welk*, *Gunsmoke*, *Bonanza*, and anything with Jim Nabors while she ate her dinner. My mother occasionally let me watch Hallmark or Disney specials, but I didn't tell anyone this. I ate up. My mother never made me pancakes on any day.

My mother didn't even ask me about Mary Alice's birthday party when she came to pick me up an hour later. She hurried out of the car and ran up the walkway while most of the other mothers sauntered and chatted leisurely with Mary Alice's mother. All these mothers looked the same, with their bright colored dresses, their frosted pink–lipsticked lips and bubble hairdos. They looked like they never worried about promotions, jobs, or money.

Mary Alice was still wearing the nightgown she called a Lanz, which I guessed was special because the other mothers grew hushed and quietly came over to examine the white rickrack at the hem.

My mother wore a gray suit and a white blouse and black pumps, and she looked like a prison warden. This on a Saturday.

"Ready?" my mother asked. When people spoke of my mother they used words like *arty* and *intellectual*, and it was never in a good way either. She didn't wear lots of makeup like other women. She only put on bright red Revlon lipstick, blotting her lips with a square of tissue or whatever old envelope she had in her purse. She hated taking too much time getting ready for anything. She quit wearing hats and gloves like other women too because she said it was silly, and in the summer it was too hot. All the other mothers wore rollers at night to do their hair like Jackie Kennedy's. I'd seen them come out in the morning for their papers, their hair still done up. My mother kept her hair short so she didn't have to curl or fuss with it and it looked as though she were always wearing a black bathing cap. She wasn't pretty the way other mothers were pretty. My mother was striking.

Now she was breathless, thanking Mary Alice's mother, then putting her arm around me as we hurried toward the car. The sun was one big white unshuttered lens in the sky. It was Indian summer, and the warm air smelled of leaves burning.

"Why are we running?"

"We're late for Tougaloo." A few of the mothers turned at the word *Tougaloo*.

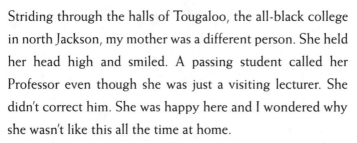

Striding through the halls of Tougaloo, the all-black college in north Jackson, my mother was a different person. She held her head high and smiled. A passing student called her Professor even though she was just a visiting lecturer. She didn't correct him. She was happy here and I wondered why she wasn't like this all the time at home.

The lecture wasn't in a classroom like I thought it would be. It was in a big auditorium and there weren't but a handful of people there, all of them black, none of them looking too thrilled to be inside, in school on Saturday morning. I could tell my mother was disappointed in the small group.

I didn't see him at first, but Perry was already there, taking pictures. He was white, but nobody took notice of him. I wondered how he did that.

I had never been to Tougaloo, and I had never sat in a room with more black people than white people, and neither had I wondered about how that might feel, being one of a few. I didn't like it one bit because there was no way to blend in.

I didn't make eye contact with anyone. I looked down at my shoes or I picked off the rest of the pink polish from my nails, while my mother showed slides of paintings of virgins, Old Testament patriarchs, bloodied St. Sebastians, and Jesuses getting beaten by the mobs. I looked up to see a few students listening. One was asleep. Her lecture was on religious icons and martyrs from the past, but it felt as if she were suggesting that this past had everything to do with our lives right then.

The students who listened sometimes nodded their heads in agreement. At the end, they clapped. Someone, not Perry, snapped a picture. I felt clearly then that the students who listened liked her and what she said, and it surprised me because it was only my mother.

Monday morning after the lecture at Tougaloo, my mother and I found the flowerpots at our front door knocked over, the dark, glossy leaves of our sasanqua bushes trampled, and the words WE'RE WATCHING painted in red on our front door. Garbage was all over our lawn and it wasn't even our garbage. We both started picking up the lawn when we saw that among the garbage was that morning's paper with my mother's picture there on the front page of the *Clarion-Ledger* under a headline that read "Local Professor Addresses All-Negro Crowd." There she was, my mom, standing in that auditorium at Tougaloo, her mouth open and her hands raised in the air as though she were speaking to a crowd of hundreds.

"Your picture's in the paper," I said. "That *should* be good."

"No," my mother said. "Not good."

Neither one of us said anything else. My mother just put her hand over her mouth. There was another, smaller photo. I looked closer. In the bigger photo my mother looked as though she were convincing a crowd of something even though she was just talking to a few people about art. I was in the smaller picture, the one with the few people there clustered together. I looked closer at my tiny figure, the only white person. I couldn't help but notice how tightly Tine's old shirt fit across my chest.

This was way after what had happened in Montgomery, when Rosa Parks refused to give up her seat to a white man, and even after the bombings, fire hoses, and police dogs in Birmingham, where Bull Connor unleashed the KKK on a group of Freedom Riders on Mother's Day.

I, for one, did not want to get involved in any of that. I just wanted to fit in to this place just as we had fit in to all the other towns we had lived in, go along like everyone else, do whatever it was we were supposed to do, let whatever was supposed to happen happen. I intended to live my life staying out of the way.

But white teachers weren't supposed to teach black students. White people weren't supposed to be among so many black people. Now all of a sudden my mother and I had jumped onto the pages of the local newspaper known by some as the *Klan-Ledger*. We were officially involved.

I ran back inside and got Perry's Pentax, adjusting the strap to fit better around me. If they had a picture of us at Tougaloo, I would take pictures of this. I took pictures of the garbage in our yard and the words splattered on our front door. Willa Mae came and the two of us finished cleaning up the yard while my mother set to work scrubbing down the front door.

Inside, when we finally ate breakfast, the phone rang. When I answered, I heard breathing, then a man's voice say, "Watch your back."

"Do I know you?" I asked, but the caller hung up.

Before I could tell my mother, the phone rang again. I picked it up on the second ring, ready to yell, but it was my grandmother. "Please remind your mother that women here should appear in print only three times in their lives: when they're born, when they get married, and when they die."

"I'll tell her."

"I imagine she's getting ready for school, so I won't bother her." I looked at my mother, who was still staring at the paper. She hadn't even turned the page. "When are you coming to visit?"

"I don't know," I said. "Soon."

"Good. I'll make all your favorites. How are you all doing on peaches?"

I opened the kitchen cupboard and saw the jars of my grandmother's pear and peach preserves, the cloves hanging, suspended in the sugary juices, just behind my grandmother's careful script. It was like having her there with us, stored away.

"Two jars left."

"I'll put away more." She stayed on the line. "I'm worried. Should I be worried?"

"I don't *think* so."

As soon as we hung up, I heard someone at the front door. I thought of the man's voice on the phone, the one who said "Watch your back." Before I could say, *Don't open the door!*, my mother opened the door and ran straight into Perry's arms. I looked at them together. When had this started? Since when did they hug like that? My mother buried her face in his neck and Perry whispered something into her ear. Even though I liked Perry, I felt queasy.

"This is all your fault," I said. "She wouldn't've even gone to Tougaloo if you hadn't told her. You took pictures. Now I bet my mom is going to lose her job."

"I didn't take that picture," Perry said quietly into my mother's hair.

"What are you talking about?" I said, pushing them apart.

"I never gave any film to that newspaper, Sam," he said.

"Besides, I never took a shot like that." He said he took close-ups of students, but there were no wide-angle photographs of crowds. He sounded calm and sure, and even though I believed him, I didn't want to.

"So how did the newspaper get those pictures?"

"I think there was a guy from the school," Perry said. "But he never said who he was with."

"We believe you, Perry," my mother said.

"They threw trash all over our yard," I said.

"I know, I know," he said. "I'm here to help."

"You don't have to, Perry, really," my mother said. "I don't want to make you late for work."

"This is bad," I said. "Miss Jenkins won't like this one bit." I realized then that I was thinking of both my school and my mother's. Who in their right mind would ever ask me to the dance now? Perry had brought nothing but trouble into both our lives. I waited, looking from Perry to my mother, the three of us just standing there, breathing.

The phone rang again and I left my mother with Perry to answer it. "What is it now?" I screamed into the receiver.

"Hi, sweetie. This is Mary Alice's mom. Is your mom there?"

"Oh, I'm so sorry, Mrs. McLemore," I said. "Let me get her."

When I ran to the front door again, my mother and Perry separated, as though they had been caught doing something.

"Mom, you have a phone call." My mother went to her room to pick up the other phone.

I listened to them talk from the kitchen phone while I watched Perry outside sweeping the walk. "I know this is a difficult time," Mrs. McLemore said, as though someone in our family had just died. "But maybe we can help." Mrs. McLemore wanted to know if we could come over for dinner in a week or so. I gently replaced the receiver and ran into my mother's room, nodding over and over, doing a silent clap as soon as she accepted the invitation.

When I sat down for lunch in the cafeteria at school, everyone stood up and left. Everyone had seen my mother in the paper. *Why did we have to eat with anyone anyway?* I tried to convince myself. Who'd made that rule? I didn't have anything to say to Mary Alice or her friends anyway. I looked around and saw Ears sitting alone, staring off and out the window. I sat across from him. He stared while I opened up my parchment paper.

"Don't you have a lunch?"

He said no. He said his father lost his job. "He joined a union. People don't like unions here. They think they're Communist. My dad's from Mississippi. He's no Russian."

"My dad's from here, too." I gave Ears half my peanut butter and banana sandwich. Then we took our minds off being hungry, reading out loud to each other from a comic book about superheroes.

After lunch we had a free period, so Ears and I stayed on the blacktop. There were still cicada shells everywhere, in the grass, and up and down tree trunks. A few were in the midst of coming out of their shells in slow motion, and it looked obscene, like you were seeing them doing something private.

"It's a K-2 sky," I said.

"What's that mean?"

"You use a K-2 yellow filter on your camera to darken the sky and bring out the clouds," I said. "Makes a better photograph. That's what my mom's friend Perry says."

Ears just nodded. "It looks cemetery out here to me."

"You mean sad?"

"That's what I said," Ears whispered to me. "Reminds me of something out of the Bible." Ears was a lot like my cousin Tine. He made me miss her.

"Which part?" I asked.

He shrugged. "That part when God gets mad?"

After that weekend the light changed altogether. Shadows crossed everything: the lawns, the houses, and the trees. In the afternoon, as I walked home from school, I marveled at how the sun lit up the tops of trees while all the undergrowth hovered in a green-black range. At home, Willa Mae and I threw open all the windows to let the cool inside.

A week after my mother's picture appeared in the paper, a week of eating lunch every day with Ears, a week of me just standing around outside or in the halls, watching everyone else go about their high school business, Mary Alice stood looking in the mirror of the girls' room, fixing her hair. She was putting her long blond hair into ponytails above her ears.

"You know my brother Stone?"

I nodded. I hoped I wasn't turning red.

"He said you were cute." She smiled, picked up her stack of books, propped them on her right hip, waved with two fingers, then twirled around and left, saying, "See you Friday at our house for dinner." Like a ballerina's, her head never moved when she walked. Mary Alice McLemore wasn't always the nicest, but she was the prettiest girl in both the ninth and tenth grade classes, and she was Stone's sister, almost entirely diminishing my competition. And he said I was cute! My luck had suddenly turned.

For the McLemores' I wore one of Tine's old red dresses. My mother wore a drippy black skirt with a knit black top. Together she hoped they looked like a black cocktail dress. She wore a string of pearls her mother had given her, and she clipped two sparkly earrings on the front of her top for decoration. To me, they looked like two earrings trying to look like something they weren't.

"That's the biggest flagpole I've ever seen," my mother said as we walked up to the McLemores' front door.

"That old thing?" Mrs. McLemore said, standing at the entrance. "Well, we're very patriotic when it comes to this state."

"Don't let her scare you away," Mr. McLemore joked. "Call me Jack." His face was red, and already he had a drink for my mother as we walked into their home. She laughed and accepted it, the ice clinking in the wet glass. "You fly yours?"

"I'm afraid not," my mother said. "Not since my husband died. Besides, we don't have a flagpole."

"I understand he died a war hero," Mr. McLemore said, quietly, in a way I appreciated.

My mother nodded.

I wanted to say something more about my dad, other than that he was dead.

"He was in charge of his own platoon," I said. "They were bringing in supplies to a village. But before, their helicopter crashed. He stayed with his soldiers until the end."

"He must have been very brave," Mrs. McLemore said. "And you must be so proud that he fought for our country."

My mother just stared off at some point beyond Mrs. McLemore.

Stone was there and so was Mary Alice. They were setting the table and pouring iced tea. They looked like they were in a television commercial. They introduced my mother to little Jeffy.

"Jeff Davies," he said. He wore plastic Slinky glasses with eyes that popped out.

"For Jefferson Davis? You're kidding, right?" my mother said, laughing. I looked at her and I tried to make my eyes say, *Can't you just pretend to be like other people? Just this once? For me?* I knew my mother was tired from her day of teaching, and already the two sips of her drink had gone to her head. Mrs. McLemore excused Jeffy so that he could go watch *The Jetsons* on TV.

"What a lovely shade," my mother said, walking into their living room.

The room had what Mrs. McLemore called lavender-colored walls, which I hoped my mother wouldn't comment on. My mother hated what people called the color lavender because she said it never looked like the real lavender. She felt the same about lilac. I thought the room was nothing but beautiful.

Mrs. McLemore said she saw the color in Natchez. She talked about Natchez—the silt, the rich alluvial soil of the delta and how it had once been the floor of the sea itself. She made me want to go there. She told my mother about their new living room ceiling covered with Armstrong Cushion to cover the cracks and stains, not knowing that my mother didn't give a hoot about such things. But I did. I wanted a house like the McLemores'.

Over their fireplace, leaning on the mantel were wooden plaques that read FAITH, HOPE, and LOVE.

Mrs. McLemore could keep a conversation going. She said that she used to love that Loretta Young. Every Sunday night she had looked forward to *The Loretta Young Show* on TV, just to watch Loretta float down that open staircase wearing a floor-length strapless gown with a full diaphanous skirt. Every Sunday night. Mrs. McLemore's pearls settled into the hollows of her collarbone while she sat for a minute, thinking about Loretta Young.

Magazines called *America* and *Commonwealth* were fanned out on the coffee table.

We all at once began to talk about how TV shows ended, how Dinah Shore blew kisses and said, "See the USA in your Chevrolet," and how Red Buttons used to soft-shoe it off the stage to his "Ho-Ho Song."

"You know what I miss?" my mother said. "I miss that Jimmy Durante show—when he ended with 'Good night, Mrs. Calabash.'"

"Isn't that Jewish?" Mrs. McLemore said.

"I hear you teach art up at the college," Stone said. Everyone went quiet. I had never before seen or heard anyone approximately my age change the subject as he had.

"Art history," my mother said.

"I don't know about all this modern art," Mrs. McLemore said. "I just know I like what I like."

"That's right, honey." Mr. McLemore poured everyone more drinks.

"Mom's hoping to take me to Europe soon," I said, trying to follow Stone's lead.

"Greece, actually," my mother said. "I used to love to travel. Anywhere. I miss it."

Mary Alice's mother said she didn't like Europe at all because she said it was too hilly. She shook her head and said it was a wonder how little old her got to travel as much as she did, but she said her husband did enough travel for the both of them. He often went on business trips to the coast and had even heard Patti Page and Peggy Lee sing.

"We saw your picture in the paper," Mary Alice said, smiling.

Mary Alice's mother shot her a look. "Don't be rude."

I loved Mrs. McLemore more than ever right then.

"What do you want to do when you get out of school, Mary Alice?" my mother asked. She always asked this of her students.

Mary Alice said she wanted to be a Delta Airlines stewardess and then a homemaker.

My mother nodded. Somehow, I knew what she was thinking. She hated them all and she thought she was better.

No one even bothered asking me what I wanted to be when I grew up. It didn't matter anyway. Wasn't I going to Randolph-Macon Women's College as my aunt had or Ole Miss as my father had and as all my cousins were surely to go? I didn't know what I wanted to be anyway. I just knew what I didn't want to be: a teacher like my mom. I didn't want to be anything like my mom. I wanted to be more like Mrs. McLemore.

"I know you think you were doing some kind of good out there at Tougaloo," Mrs. McLemore said in a newly serious way. "But you're just wasting your time."

"I just don't understand why they have to get all riled up," Mr. McLemore said. "They don't have such bad lives. Our Mattie's happy. Go and ask her yourself."

Mattie was their maid. Mary Alice said Mattie did every-thing—cooked, cleaned, and even made out the grocery lists. "If she had front teeth, she'd be real pretty," Mary Alice said. Mary Alice wore a charm bracelet that jingled each time she passed around the deviled ham and cheese on crackers.

"Oh, don't get me wrong," Mrs. McLemore went on, look-ing into her glass. "The coloreds serve a purpose here. Unlike the Chinese." She put one manicured fingernail in the drink and came out with a gnat, and then rolled it between her fingers.

"And now they want to integrate into our schools," Mr. McLemore said. "They're just going to ruin things for our children."

"I don't see how that can ruin things," my mother started.

"The quality of our schools will plummet if we agree to integration. Don't you want your daughter to have all the advantages that you didn't?" Mrs. McLemore asked my mother.

My mother smiled. I braced myself and only wished Mrs. McLemore knew to do the same. "What makes you think I didn't have all the advantages?" My mother paused to breathe and look steadily into Mrs. McLemore's eyes the way she did sometimes with me to make me listen. "And why would you think that having advantages makes a bit of difference in the formation of a human being?"

Mrs. McLemore looked up and down and all around my mother. Her eyes couldn't settle down.

"Did we mention we knew your husband's people, the Russells?" Mr. McLemore said, patting his wife's knee. He talked about my great-grandfather Frank Russell, who had once been a schoolteacher. Frank Russell and his father had helped settle parts of Smith County, and he sold goods he brought up from New Orleans in his wagon. I was surprised Mr. McLemore knew so much about my father's relatives.

"The Russells are all buried in a pretty little cemetery on the property where my husband grew up," my mother said. "Sam has spent a lot of time out there with her grandparents."

Mrs. McLemore smiled. "It's important to know your family tree."

"She's a regular little Mississippi girl," Mr. McLemore said, squeezing my shoulder. I don't know why, but I breathed a sigh of relief, as though I'd passed some test. I didn't think my mother had, though.

I watched Stone watching my mother, who smiled and said nothing more. Stone had Elvis lips, but his eyes weren't so boyish or sad.

At the dinner table I sat next to Stone and I tried to keep breathing to steady my heart. We all held hands to say grace. His palms were hard and cool. His big hands with long, slender fingers were just turning into man hands. I had never held a boy's hand in any religious or romantic way before. My knee brushed against his.

Mr. McLemore poured my mother another drink. We ate roast with pearl onions, scalloped potatoes, and tomato aspic with olives and celery. My mother and I never ate like this on a weeknight, and I had never seen anyone cut his meat the way Mr. McLemore did, holding his fork like a dagger and then sawing away with his knife. Stone did the same. I thought of how my father had cut his meat, all the power coming from the tips of his fingers.

We used colored paper napkins too. At home my mother and I each had our own cloth napkin that we only washed once a week. I thought now how disgusting that might be to some.

No one spoke while we ate. My mother insisted on conversations at the table. She asked the McLemores what they had done that summer. I tried not to notice my mother watching Stone waving his fork as he spoke. I just listened. He had been to the bridge over the East Pascagoula, even fished in the same spot where those two shipyard workers said space aliens abducted them. He told us about the Mississippi Gulf Coast, where they went for family vacations, the alligator and turtle races in Long Beach, the Deer Ranch, and his favorite, Beauvoir, Jefferson Davis's house in Biloxi.

If my dad were alive, I would tell him about Stone. In my mind, we all would have gotten along.

Stone and his father said something to each other that sounded like gibberish but was really just man talk, separating themselves for a moment from the rest of us.

I was glad not to be a boy in Mississippi. Boys couldn't just be smart. They had to be smart in school, then pretend to be hunters and farmers even if they weren't. They had to say "ain't" and use the wrong verbs every now and then, just to show others they hadn't gotten beyond their raising. If boys were smart they had to be two people all the time.

"What, are you two in a klavern or something?" my mother said. She sounded drunk and she kept smiling, giggling even. When they were together, my mother and Perry often made fun of the KKK and all that was happening. They said laughing about it helped them get through a day of listening to crazy people. "You aren't Kluckers, are you?"

Mr. McLemore cleared his throat. Mrs. McLemore disappeared into the kitchen to get something.

"Ma'am?" Stone asked, filling my mother's water glass.

My mother and Perry had gotten too used to mocking anything having to do with the Ku Klux Klan; it had become habit. Once she'd told me, "The whole thing is so barbaric and so absurd."

"Mom?"

"I'm fine," she whispered, then quietly hiccupped. "I'll behave. I promise." She began drinking water.

I excused myself, thinking I was going to be sick. I couldn't watch Stone or Mary Alice watching my mother and me as if we were some free freak show at their dinner table. And I didn't want to stick around to see what wrong thing my mother would do or say next. Luckily, I knew where to find the air-raid shelter bathroom, so I knew where to hide in order to collect and prepare myself for the worst, which was my mother after three drinks. This was so much worse than a nuclear bomb explosion.

In the downstairs powder room, I splashed cold water on my face. I took three deep breaths. When I opened the door, Stone was there.

"There you are," he said. "I've been looking for you."

"You have?"

He smiled. "Sure I have." He stepped closer, closer than any boy had ever stepped. "Hey."

"Hey," I said, swallowing.

"Samantha." He called me by my full name like that and then stepped even closer. "I was wondering. Will you come to the dance with me?"

This moment felt so new, I wished it would slow down. I wished I had time to step back and look at it from a distance, with a long, wide-angle lens. This handsome boy I admired and liked to look at appeared before me just like that, as though he had dropped down from outer space, and there we were, face-to-face in his air raid shelter, safe from the Russians and all the other grownups. He had asked me and I would say yes and we would be going to the dance. Me. Samantha Thomas would be going to a high school dance with Stone McLemore.

"Sure," I said, trying to sound as casual as you please. But it came out sounding like a cough.

He lifted my chin the way handsome men did to pretty women in the movies. He closed his eyes. I had never before seen a boy up close with his eyes closed. It felt private and personal, and I held my breath so I wouldn't mess up this perfect moment. We kissed, and I hoped I wouldn't burp up the onions from dinner. When I opened my eyes, he saw and stopped.

"You're supposed to keep your eyes shut," he whispered.

"I didn't know."

He smiled. "You're like some kind of purebred. My dad's told me all about your family. I think my kin might even have known your kin way back."

For some reason I remembered just then that I was wearing Tine's old red dress. Tine drooled when she was nervous. I hoped I wasn't drooling all over myself.

I could hear Mrs. McLemore in the living room upstairs, saying that we weren't required to obey northern laws.

When we went back up separately, I couldn't stop smiling. Not even the sound of Mary Alice's charm bracelet tinkling could wipe away my grin.

My mother was saying that Mississippi had isolated itself from the rest of the nation.

"It's not a separate nation-state," she said. She was no longer jumbling her words. She had her teacher voice on. I wasn't sure which was worse. "It's not like we're unaccountable to a higher authority. If that's the case, then we're living in a totalitarian state."

"You sure do have some ideas," Mr. McLemore said, grinning.

"I didn't understand a word you just said," Mrs. McLemore said, laughing, fanning herself with her napkin. "Mary Alice, clear those dishes, would you, dear? Jeffy, quit running around. You're wearing out my last nerve."

"Your husband's family, they're fine people, good people, your husband's people." Mr. McLemore's voice went low and soft. "I just know they don't want you agitating and stirring up trouble here where you're trying to start a new life and all."

My mother and Mr. McLemore stared at each other then and something happened between them. Something understood just between the two of them. My mother nodded. "Thank you for the advice." Then she turned to me. "Sam, we should be going." She wasn't serious rude. Just serious polite.

As we were leaving, Mr. McLemore took my mother's elbow and drew her close. "Honey, this isn't your fight." He was almost close enough to kiss her. "Let's us leave the serious business of governing to our governor."

My mother just smiled. "As long as the governor works for us."

Already little Jeffy had turned on the TV. A previously recorded performance was on *The Ed Sullivan Show*, and even though the McLemores' TV was the biggest I'd seen, that box didn't seem like it could hold the sounds coming out of Louis Armstrong's trumpet.

When we got back home from the McLemores', my mother pulled off her black shirt and skirt. It seemed she couldn't get out of those clothes fast enough. She pulled on one of my dad's old shirts to sleep in, and for a change she climbed into my bed with one of her big art books. She was so caught up in her books—huge picture books of art and art history, books two times the size of her head. She once told me she got hooked on art because every year her mother gave her a big art book for Christmas. My mother loved art and sometimes talked about old paintings like they were old friends. She told me that when she was my age, looking through her art books was an escape, and when she looked hard enough and long enough at the pictures, she was where she wanted to be. Now every night when she climbed into bed, sometimes even when it was still light outside, she'd haul these books in with her, opening them on a pillow so the corners wouldn't jab into her stomach, then with a pencil behind her ear and a notepad nearby, she would read these books, even the captions, and study the pictures until she had them memorized.

She had seen the Acropolis only in pictures. She was reading about Hadrian's Villa at Tivoli. She had just finished rereading Euripides. She wanted to do a study on all the different versions of Aphrodite and what every culture from different times saw as beauty.

When I climbed in beside her, she turned off the light. I couldn't stop thinking of Stone. He had kissed me. My first kiss and it was from Stone McLemore. Lying there next to my mother's warm, soft body made me feel weird.

"Kitty-cat," she said, tracing the outline of my ear. She sounded a little drunk.

"Quit it."

"Pookie-poo." I could smell the wine on her breath and the Pond's cold cream on her face.

"Why do you have to be so strange, Mom?"

She was laughing and I was not.

"Because that's the way God made me." She was making a joke, imitating someone now, but I didn't know whom. A McLemore?

"Are you making fun of them?"

"I wouldn't be at all surprised if each of them had white sheets and hoods in their closets. They are as bad as the people who painted our front door." She picked up some of my hair and twirled it around. I batted away her hand.

"Stone is not a member of the KKK, Mom."

"Honey," she sighed. "Don't go falling for a boy like Stone. He's not our kind."

"Leave me alone, Mom." Our kind? What was that supposed to mean? I didn't care if Mary Alice or Stone was our kind, but I sure knew I wanted to be Stone's kind. I thought of the whole McLemore world that had just opened up to me. It was a family world where they took vacations together, ate casseroles, held hands and said grace. I had never been skiing, but for some reason the McLemores looked like people who skied or who would eventually ski.

"You don't need their acceptance," my mother said.

I thought about that. "Yes, I do." I said it the way women say it at their weddings. "I do."

"You really don't, sweetie. You shouldn't."

I looked at her. I hadn't even told my mother about Stone's kissing me or asking me to the dance. This was my first secret from her, and it didn't feel right.

"When did you know?" I said. "About Dad. When did you know he was 'the one'?"

"I had no idea I would marry your father," she said. "But there was no way I could live without him." She stopped, thinking about what she had said. "Now I suppose we both have to, huh?" There was a pause. "When you were a baby, I'd pick you up and you'd put your hand inside my hair and you'd keep it there."

"Mom," I said. "I just want to sleep."

She took out her hearing aid. She unhooked the string of pearls around her neck. I used to like playing with this necklace and would until she made me stop. She picked up the framed picture of my father from my nightstand and stared at it.

Mary Alice told us girls at school that sometimes her mother declared a "pajama day" and they both stayed in their pajamas all day and watched TV and played board games and anything else you could do in bed. They ate meals on trays and had lots of girl talk. Oh, how we all envied Mary Alice.

After my mother finally left my room, I listened to her mumbling to herself in her bedroom. I knew she was talking to my dad. For my mother, my dad was always there with us. For me he was gone most of the time, except when I chose to think of him. I wondered, had she married him just to leave home? And now was she looking to leave again, this time with Perry? I rolled over and faced the wall, half wishing she'd come back.

CHAPTER 5

IN THE FOLLOWING WEEKS my mother kept getting anonymous letters in the mail, and she wouldn't let me read them. Then, after she listened to one nasty phone call, she told Willa Mae I was no longer allowed to answer the phone. One morning, when I came back from my daily picture-taking walk, I found a black cat lying dead on top of our newspaper outside our front door. My mother put a stop to my early-morning photo sessions, so I started taking pictures after school.

If this part of my life had been a short-answer test like the ones we took at school, some of the questions would have been these: What would my dad say to all this? What was the right thing to do and when would I know it? Would he want us to stay here in his home state, or go, just go? Would leaving mean running away? Or, would he want us to stay here, close to his family?

Perry came and put new bolt locks on our doors. At night, he came by to check on us. He looked tired and sweaty, his shirttails hanging out, but he always smiled and made my mother laugh. He brought photography books for me to look through too, pointing out pictures taken by "famous" people I'd never heard of: Alfred Eisenstaedt, Ansel Adams, Margaret Bourke-White, Robert Capa, Walker Evans, and Dorothea Lange.

Perry was the only white person I knew who lived in an all-black neighborhood. Every day after he finished teaching, he taught kids in his neighborhood about photography. He was helping their parents register to vote too.

Every few days I gave my film to Perry and we stood side by side in his darkroom, developing pictures. Sometimes he talked while he worked, telling me how important it was to stay alert for good photographs, how to really *look* and *see*, or how he thought these difficult times in Mississippi were probably his most productive period. Once he got all worked up, saying that being here was better than the riots he'd photographed. No way was he budging. No way was he leaving.

"I'm finally *part* of a place," he said that afternoon. "I'm not just taking pictures." I couldn't help but think how I didn't feel quite the same way yet about living in Jackson.

This was in the fall of 1962, when winter was coming up on all of us. Weeks went by and then the leaves on the trees and the leaves on the ground were all washed in gold and burgundy and that's all you saw. Then *finally* people seemed to forget about my mother guest lecturing at Tougaloo, because there was other news.

A black twenty-nine-year-old air force veteran named James Meredith had enrolled at the University of Mississippi, or "Ole Miss," in Oxford as a transfer student, and at the end of September, on a beautiful warm Sunday night, in front of a building called the Lyceum, middle-aged men who didn't want Meredith attending an all-white university egged on students to attack the National Guards President Kennedy had sent down. There they all were at our state's institution for higher learning, running around in tear gas smoke, billy-clubbing one another before their first day of classes. My mother and I watched it all on TV and we both knew that this marked the beginning or end of something, though we weren't sure of what.

In a televised address to the state of Mississippi, President Kennedy said to us, "If this country should ever reach the point where any man or any group of men, by force or threat of force, could long defy the commands of our court and

Constitution, then no law would stand free from doubt, no judge would be sure of his right, and no citizen would be safe from his neighbor."

Governor Ross Barnett addressed the state too, saying, "We must either submit to the unlawful dictates of the federal government or stand up like men and tell them 'NEVER!'"

It took three or four U.S. marshals just to get James Meredith to his first class the following day, a class that happened to be Colonial American History.

None of the business with James Meredith especially interested other kids at my school because it was all happening up in Oxford, which might as well have been Mars—plus all the girls in my class were now wearing bras, all, that is, except me. Mary Alice had started something and every girl at Jackson High School wanted to be like Mary Alice McLemore.

Even though she had already agreed to get me one, my mother said she could not understand what my rush was. Besides, she said, she was teaching all day every day that week, and she had a "slew" of faculty meetings every afternoon and she couldn't get home until after the stores all closed. So she asked Willa Mae to please walk me into town and take me to get fitted.

Willa Mae knew where to go, but I didn't. I had never been downtown with Willa Mae before. At home Willa Mae was the boss of me. At home she didn't have to call me Miss Samantha either. She drank iced tea or water not from a mayonnaise jar like other maids but from one of our own drinking glasses, and she shared our bathroom.

Downtown was different. Because she was black, Willa Mae wasn't allowed to go into the white stores without me. Because she was black, she couldn't try on hats or use the restrooms. Because she was black, she couldn't say *Yeah* or *Yes, Bob*. She had to say *Yes, ma'am* or *Yes, sir,* or *Yes, Mr. Smith*. Because she was black, she might have to step off the sidewalk to make way for a white person and use separate waiting areas and drinking fountains marked COLORED.

These were the rules. Right or wrong, this was just the way things were. Even though I had been taught that everybody was a human being and that everybody had the same rights because we lived in America and equality was what America was all about, I still had to follow rules.

Already I was in the habit of taking Perry's Pentax with me most everywhere I went. It was fast becoming my camera. I had adjusted the strap and it fit around me just so. I took pictures of all the stores that sold candy, talcum powder, Moon Pies, and bubblegum. Then finally, we got to the window with the mannequins wearing girdles.

Willa Mae came into the store with me and sat in a chair beside the door, waiting, as a big-bosomed saleswoman helped me find the right size and fit.

First I tried on a white bra over my shirt. The saleswoman frowned and said that it would be impossible to judge the fit that way. Willa Mae sucked her tooth and said something like, "If there's nothing to judge, you can't judge."

The saleswoman looked at Willa Mae, smiled, then led me into the changing room, insisting on staying as I took off my shirt. She said so much depended on *how* I put a bra on.

She said you were certainly *not* supposed to snap it on, then twist it around and pull it up the way I saw my mother do every single day. The saleswoman showed me how you were supposed to bend and carefully put yourself into the thing, assuming you had something to put in.

I did what she told me to do and when I stood up straight, she said, "See?" The fit was no different and it was still uncomfortable, but I kept it on anyway, and I paid her the money. I had to have a bra. I just had to.

It was hot. And Willa Mae and I still had the walk back home.

"Come on," I said. Wearing the bra made my back feel straighter, and I held my head higher. "I still have enough money to get us some sodas. The drugstore is just up the street."

I liked going into the drugstore, where the bottles and boxes stood in neat rows, organized by varying heights, the prices clearly marked so you wouldn't even have to touch a thing, just look.

When we got inside and at the counter, I turned to Willa Mae. "What would you like?"

"A Mr. Coca-Cola, please," she said to me. Willa Mae didn't even feel she could say, *A Coca-Cola, please.* She thought she had to put a Mr. or a Mrs. in front of everything. That wasn't like her at all. It was like she was acting while we were downtown, and she knew I knew.

"Please what?" the woman behind the counter said.

"We'll have two Coca-Colas, please," I said.

"Please what?" The woman behind the counter wasn't looking at me. She was looking at Willa Mae.

Willa Mae stared at her shoes.

"I'm talking to you, girl."

It occurred to me only then that this woman wanted Willa Mae to call me Miss. She wanted Willa Mae to redo her sentence. She wanted Willa Mae to say, *A Mr. Coca-Cola, please, Miss Samantha.* If Willa Mae were to do that right then, well, that would have been impossible, not for her maybe, but for me. In our house, Willa Mae was boss. Here in town, it was hard enough to pretend otherwise, but to go that far, to have Willa Mae say to me, *please, Miss Samantha,* we both would have bust a gut laughing.

I looked at the woman behind the counter. I had on my new bra and it felt to me like a bulletproof vest pinching me to do something. "Of all the people in here, I'm the girl, and I asked for two Coca-Colas. Please."

The woman stared at me for a beat, then got two bottles out of the cooler. She opened them on the counter, all the while keeping an eye on Willa Mae, who never looked up. I got two straws.

"She needs to take hers outside," the woman said. For a brief instant, I saw Willa Mae glance up at her. It was an expression I recognized.

Once not long before, when we first moved into town, Willa Mae and I were walking back from the park when we stopped at a gas station at the corner for water. There was a drinking fountain there that was part of the soda machine. There were no signs, but it was understood, white people drank from the fountain, and because there was only the one water fountain, black people had to get a used soda bottle from the empties stacked there, fill the bottle with water, then drink from the used bottle. But after I drank from the fountain, Willa Mae drank right after me, just as I had done. We weren't thinking.

Another boy not much older than me saw Willa Mae do this and said, "You better get you a bottle next time, girl, or else there won't be a next time."

Willa Mae looked at that white boy and then quickly looked down at her feet. But I saw what was in her eyes and I felt the sting of her shame then, not for herself, not even for me, but for that little white boy. She knew what he would likely become.

Willa Mae had that same look in her eyes then, when she looked back up at the woman behind the counter.

I put my camera on my hip and tried snapping a picture of the woman without her noticing. She noticed and called for her supervisor.

I looked out the window. Outside, across the street, a group of black people were gathered. I did a double-take. They weren't just gathering to talk. This group of black people wore posterboards around their necks: YOUR CONSIDERATION CAN HELP US END RACIAL SEGREGATION, one posterboard said. Another read JOIN US IN OUR FIGHT FOR FREEDOM. They walked past the movie theater where *The Day Mars Invaded Earth* was showing.

I walked closer to the window to watch white men begin to gather in the street. They were yelling at the group of black people, but I couldn't hear what they were saying.

Willa Mae tapped my shoe with her shoe, and then motioned toward the door.

"One minute," I whispered. "Please?"

A group of four or five college students and what looked to be their professors, black and white, came into the drugstore and sat down at the end of the counter, all quiet and business-like. They waited to order, but the woman behind the counter did not move from where she stood near me.

All of the other white people seated at the counter stopped talking and stood up. They put their money down, leaving full plates of burgers and fries, and then they left, mumbling and shaking their heads. Willa Mae and I both could feel something happening then, except I could tell that she wanted to leave and I wanted to stay.

The place began to fill up. The angry white men from outside came inside, yelling now at the black and white students and professors sitting together at the lunch counter. These angry white men used every word I was never allowed to use, and then some. Three policemen came in too. They stood by, listened, and watched. I knew what they knew. Black and white people were not allowed to sit together at any lunch counter in Jackson, Mississippi.

Just then I thought about the samurai warriors I read about in *National Geographic* and how they prepared themselves for battle by deciding that they were dead already so they had nothing to lose. Had my father done that? What was the right thing to do now? Was this feeling I had now what he'd meant when he said "You'll know"? I kept the camera at my hip and snapped more pictures. The yelling inside around the lunch counter was loud enough now so that no one heard my camera clicking.

Willa Mae stood against the wall close to the door. I could tell by her eyes that she had gone somewhere deep within herself, as if willing herself to disappear. We were the same like that.

One of the black women seated at the counter was a tall,

pretty college-aged woman who carried a purse and two books. She could have been one of my mother's students, except that she was black. She stared down at the space on the counter in front of her, saying nothing.

"You've got to learn to see," Perry Walker had said to me, loading my camera with film. "The camera is gonna record whatever it's aimed at. It's up to you to pick what you want to record."

I brought my camera to my right eye, then closed my left, and from then on, the me that was me was gone and I was just seeing, watching everything through that lens. Mostly, I kept my focus on this girl, so pretty and so calm, staring down at a full glass of water somebody else had left behind.

Old and young white men closed in on that small group at the counter, and their focus was the same as mine. They called the girl names. She said nothing. The people at the counter with her said nothing. The white men standing behind her poured ketchup and then sugar over her head. She did nothing. The people at the counter with her did nothing. Young men gathered to jeer and gape, their cigarettes dangling from their lips. One punched her arm. She fixed her eyes on the lunch counter or on the glass of water—I couldn't tell which. She did nothing. If I had been her, sitting there, while all those nasty white boys poured a mess over my head, saying all those mean things, would I have been able to keep my cool like that? I thought of what gave her courage. She wanted to sit at the counter, but I also knew there was more. She wanted what I had and what I didn't even think twice about. She wanted to live her life, just like me and everybody else.

Those white men and boys were attacking her and she'd done nothing, but just by *being* there, by sitting there where she was not supposed to be sitting, she was doing something. They were screaming and getting so angry, their faces turned red. They made so much noise and their voices were so loud, you had to go quiet. I kept my eye behind the camera and snapped picture after picture. Then I quit taking pictures of what was happening. I took pictures of the crowd of angry white men yelling at the people at the lunch counter sitting there doing nothing. There were others in the crowd watching what was happening. They could have been looking at a circus performance or a child's running race. They were smiling and cheering. They shared cigarettes. They were having a good time.

The policemen stood by and watched.

There we all were in a town some called "A Fine Family Place," a town Miss Jenkins said William Tecumseh Sherman had burned to the ground ninety-nine years ago. Maybe we should have just left it that way.

I was still taking the pictures, my right eye glued to my camera, when I saw him, Stone. His face was one of the angry faces I snapped. He saw me and squeezed through the crowd, asking me what I was doing there.

"There's nothing here for you but *trouble*," he said in a voice not at all like his. "Now go. Go."

"Why are *you* here? What are you doing?" I was shouting over the crowd now. My voice barely carried. There was a lot of pushing and shoving. I felt a hand on my arm. It was Willa Mae pulling me toward the door. When I turned back around, Stone was gone.

Outside, men were swinging baseball bats and billy clubs at black women carrying handbags and wearing white kid gloves. These women were all dressed up to go shopping, and these men came out of the drugstore and charged at them because . . . because I don't know why. Because they were angry white men? That was all there was to it, all I could think of, and it was nothing but *wrong*.

Willa Mae and I were both of the crowd and separated from the crowd. We were outside, our backs up against the building. I stepped forward and started taking pictures again. On what, on whom, and where to focus: it was like my camera knew what to do and I was just following its lead. People were yelling, their voices shouting, "They're not going to eat with us and they're not going to vote with us!"

"Your mother will kill us both if we don't get out of here." Willa Mae's voice rose above all the noise.

I rewound the film in my camera the way Perry taught me, unloaded the exposed film and put it in my pocket, then loaded a new roll. The drugstore waitress from behind the counter ran out shouting to a policeman that I had taken pictures and that I was "one of them outside agitators." The policeman headed toward me. When he caught up with me, he yelled for me to hand over my film.

For a scary moment I didn't know what to do. My heart was thumping. Could the policeman hear it? I thought of taking off, running as fast and as far as I could. I wiped the sweat from my palms on my shirt. I didn't hold my breath but tried to breathe, then lifted my camera to my right eye and snapped a picture of his angry face.

"Yessir," I said. I rewound the film, opened my camera, unloaded, and then gave him the roll with the one shot of himself, the full roll still safe in my pocket. The policeman walked away, stuffing the roll of film in his pocket.

Willa Mae stepped away from the drugstore and joined me. We hurried from the policeman. All around us men in pickup trucks drove past, their guns visible. People didn't show their guns, especially in town. You only saw guns when men went out hunting deer, rabbits, or squirrels.

Willa Mae touched me on the arm and said, "This way."

She led me to a shortcut back toward our subdivision. Finally, when we were clear of the town and the crowd, we slowed to a walk and then caught our breath. I rearranged my camera strap around my neck and tugged at my new bra. Willa Mae kept looking behind us.

I was still scared, but then my fear turned to anger. Why

did these white people who had houses and cars, jobs and families, hate black people who were trying to make something of their lives or who looked to have nothing? I understood jealousy just fine, but this? Did it make them feel more important to hate? Something else must be at stake— something I couldn't see before me there in that store on that street in this town. They were scared of something bigger.

Being black or white wasn't supposed to make any difference. That's what I had been taught by my mother and my father both. This was so easy to say. Now I was realizing that it was a lie. And the rules, the rules I was supposed to follow, went against what we believed.

"Don't be scared," Willa Mae said.

I looked at her. "Aren't you scared?"

Willa Mae looked at me and said, "Shoot. Only thing I'm afraid of is that I'm going to do something I'll regret." We kept walking. In my mind I could still hear the sounds of people yelling "They're not going to eat with us and they're not going to vote with us!"

"Being scared is just one more thing to turn into what you want it to be," Willa Mae said. "The thing with fear is, it's like anger. You've got to change it into something else. Make it your weapon. Some can just turn it into smarts. The best of 'em can turn fear and anger into love." She looked out toward our neighborhood. "I'm not there yet."

"Have you ever voted?" I asked. She and I both knew there weren't many black people registered to vote in Mississippi.

I had never seen Willa Mae laugh out loud, but she laughed then and I saw that she was missing her side teeth. Willa Mae didn't usually look people in the eye, but she looked at me then.

"I tried to vote once," she said. "Clerk asked me how many bubbles it took to make a bar of soap. I thought it was one of those trick questions, and I said bubbles don't make soap, soap makes bubbles. He said I was wrong and I couldn't vote."

"What do soap bubbles have to do with voting?" I asked. "Did you ask?"

"Ask? I don't ask nothin'." She sounded mad. "I am colored. I am a colored woman. That's what I am."

I stopped myself from saying *I know how you feel* because what did I know? What could I know what it would be like to be black? To be the only girl in this white-personed world who was black? Would I ever really know what it was to step off a sidewalk to allow another person to pass because of her skin color?

I felt like I didn't know a darned thing. Seven years before, a Negro boy my age from Chicago had been tortured, tied to a cotton gin machinery fan, shot, and found later at the bottom of the Tallahatchie River. Even though nobody I knew in Mississippi spoke his name, news of Emmett Till gradually traveled to me and to Tine, but we never really could get anything more out of our parents. They held back as they did on most things that were happening. Now I supposed I knew why. To think on such dark happenings was almost more than a body could stand.

It started to rain, and Willa Mae and I made a run for the house. I was shivering, and even though I know she didn't believe me, I told Willa Mae it wasn't because I was scared.

CHAPTER 6

"I KNOW YOU'RE BUSY AND I KNOW WE JUST DID THIS, but would you help me develop my film?" I asked. Perry Walker and I were standing in the hall outside my mother's office at the college while she sat grading papers.

He didn't hesitate. "Let's go."

We worked side by side in his darkroom. All along his shelves were cameras of every shape and size. I picked up a particularly small one, one I hadn't noticed before. Perry nodded and smiled.

"That little puppy's a gem," he said of his smallest camera. I brought it to my eye while he talked. "It's perfect for when you want to take pictures and go unnoticed. I used that to shoot a military hospital in D.C. Two full pages in *Life*. The nurses didn't even know I was taking pictures."

Before when we developed pictures together, I'd watched him while he did most of the work. This time, he watched me.

"My dad gave me my first camera when I was eleven," he told me. He pointed to a big old black camera on the shelf. I thought better than to touch it. "It was just after the war, when rations were over and people had more money and buying a camera was all the sudden possible." In this darkroom, Perry was more than likable. Maybe because he was teaching me something. Maybe because my mother wasn't a part of the picture.

"I can't even tell what this is a picture of," I said, watching one of the photographs develop in a pan of water. We both stood back for a minute, watching the pictures form in the trays full of chemicals. The wavy figures emerged under the water, and then we hung the pictures out to dry.

"Forget about wondering what the picture is *of*. Think about what it's *about*."

"They're just snapshots," I said.

"Snapshots are the best," he said. He talked to me about looking even before I took the shot. He told me about finding the light source by looking *around*, because it is not always right in front of you. "Find the shadows," he said. "Know where your light is coming from. Maybe the only difference between snapshots and photographs people call 'art' is intention."

"I don't know what that means, but when I was snapping those pictures, it felt a little like I was spying."

"Nothing wrong with a little snooping, as long as it serves a purpose," he said. "My buddy called it soul stealing."

"Gee." I looked closer at one picture in particular. It really was Stone McLemore at the drugstore, even though I was trying to convince myself that he hadn't really been there, that I had just imagined it.

Both of us looked at all the pictures hanging like wash on a line.

"All these?" He pointed to the pictures I'd taken at the lunch counter. "They tell a story." He talked about multiple or sequential images. He said that response to a particular image is always influenced by what we see before and after it.

"This one," he said, pointing to one that I could barely look at now. It was a picture of a boy dumping a load of sugar and ketchup over the head of that girl. "You got the shot right there," Perry said. "Man, girl. You really captured something here too," he said, pointing to another. "A person can shoot from her head and she can shoot from her heart. The best pictures are shot from both. That's what you got. Jeez." I liked it best when he didn't lecture. I liked it when he quit talking all arty-farty.

Then Perry and I looked closely at another picture, a

close-up of the waitress. If somebody asked what hate looked like, I'd give him this picture. I had not known it then, but I had taken a picture of hate. Hate looked like that woman behind the lunch counter, her eyes, the lines around her mouth and nose so full of the intention to hate.

"Way to stay with the story," Perry said. There was admiration in his voice. Even I could hear that. "You got a good eye. I think I know an editor who would like this one." He pointed to the shot of the waitress. "Can I send it to him?"

"You'd do that?"

"Only with your permission."

I hesitated, for me, for my mother, for Willa Mae, for us all. I shook my head. "No," I said. Maybe I was making a mistake. Maybe giving permission to print the pictures was the right thing to do, but it was too dangerous. We didn't need any more scary phone calls or hate mail, and besides, once the pictures ran, what would Mary Alice think? And would Stone still like me? Even though I wasn't certain why Stone was at the drugstore that day, he *had* been concerned about me and my safety. Maybe he just happened to be there, getting a Coca-Cola, just as Willa Mae and I had done that day. I couldn't help myself. I still wanted Stone McLemore to like me.

"I understand," Perry said. "It's asking a lot. But that camera? My Pentax? It's yours now."

"Are you kidding?"

"No joke. You've earned it."

At school Miss Jenkins would not allow us students to discuss protesting or what had happened downtown at the drugstore, even though everyone was beginning to whisper about it. Instead, she gave us a brief lecture about how red birds and black birds don't mix. "God didn't want it that way," she said. At lunch, I overheard our principal talking to another teacher in the hall. "Lincoln educated himself by candlelight with borrowed books," he said. "Why do these little darkies want so much?"

For three weeks in October we got out of school early not because of anything that was happening around us in Jackson but because of what was going on in other parts of the world. Everyone in our school had to carry Clorox bottles filled with water and canned goods in duffel bags to better prepare ourselves for a nuclear strike because of something that had to do with Cuba and the Kennedys and a man named Castro. No matter how many times my mother rinsed the Clorox bottles, she could never quite get rid of the taste of bleach.

The neighborhoods around Jackson began to look worse and worse. One afternoon, Willa Mae and I were both sitting in the back seat, flipping through magazines with pretty houses on the covers while my mother drove Willa Mae home. As we neared Willa Mae's neighborhood, we glanced out the car windows, looking all around us. The paved roads needed fixing and the dirt roads needed paving. Some of the houses we passed were burned out or falling down. We all grew very quiet. When my mother stopped the car, I didn't want Willa Mae to get out.

"Seems like nothing's getting safer or better," I said. "Seems like everything's getting worse."

"Maybe that's what's gotta happen," Willa Mae said. She picked up her pocketbook and opened the car door. "Maybe everything's gotta break loose and fall apart before we can put it back together again right."

I stared down at the magazine in my lap. On the cover was a pretty porch with gingham-covered cushions. Everything about the picture said to me, *Here is a good place and a good life.* But that's not what I saw outside our car window. That's not what I saw Willa Mae walking toward.

Perry was having a tough time selling his photographs. He said editors were no longer interested in the "race problem," which was too "local" and "minor." The crisis in Cuba had taken over most of the front-page news. With more time and fewer deadlines, Perry relaxed. He came over at least once a week now for dinner, as if he was my mother's new best friend, and he took us out for long car drives. Every now and then we would stop at a lake, or a church, or an old share-cropper's house and Perry and I would get out of the car and spend time taking pictures. During those drives, from the back seat I watched my mother slide over up front to ride closer to Perry. I quit feeling queasy seeing them close together during these drives. I took snapshots—close-ups of Perry's arm around my mother's back, the locks on the car doors, and incidental tears in the vinyl seats.

I was still young enough to *want* to dress up for Halloween but old enough not to talk about it. I was supposed to be too old for that sort of thing. So that year, on that Halloween, I just answered the door, and under the yellow porch light I gave out our usual handfuls of candy corn.

Right after a clutch of witches and one wolf left, their parents waving from the sidewalk, I shut the door and then heard a car screech. Doors opened and slammed shut. Something exploded. I looked outside. Our mailbox was on fire. My mother called the police, but by the time they got there, we had put the fire out. The police told my mother it was just another Halloween trick, nothing they could do.

When the police left, someone threw a rock through our front window. We taped the gaping hole with cardboard from an old cut-up box, and this time we didn't even bother calling the police. Instead, I asked my mother to call Perry Walker. "Tell him to come over."

"I'm on my way," he said.

My mother and I both felt safer when Perry came over.

In state history Miss Jenkins told us that before the war, Mississippi was the fifth richest state in the Union and the only reason "we" didn't have Memphis was because the original surveyors were drunk. She quoted one line a Mississippi writer named William Faulkner wrote, that Mississippi began in the lobby of a Memphis, Tennessee, hotel called the Peabody and ran south all the way to the Gulf of Mexico.

"Mississippi really starts in Memphis," she said. "Everybody knows that." She paused then and looked at us all for a long, hard moment. "Southerners built America. Southerners are true patriots. Race mixers want to destroy the South and America."

At lunch Ears had two baloney sandwiches, each made with lots of yellow mustard, one of which he gave to me, and I just about died and went to heaven. We ate my peanut butter sandwich as a dessert while we continued reading out loud from a Captain Fantastic comic. Ears was fast becoming a better reader.

My mother signed up to chaperone our fall dance, and when she told Perry, he asked if he could attend as her date so that he could take pictures. Perry was at our house having dinner again. He fixed our window. I knew that he came over so often because he felt responsible for our safety. Maybe my mother knew that too. Maybe she liked finally having a guardian, someone looking after us. We were sort of like a family.

That night my mother laughed. "So we won't really be *together* together. You'll be the official photographer."

He smiled. "Right."

"We'll even go in separate cars. I'll take Sam."

"No!"

They both looked at me.

"I've got a ride. Stone's coming to pick me up. He just got his driver's permit."

"Whoa," Perry said, smiling. "A *date* date."

My mother stopped smiling. "You could have asked me."

"Stone," Perry said. "That's really his name?"

"Please, Mom?"

"You'll be chaperoning," Perry said to my mother. "And I'll be taking pictures. We'll *both* be watching." Perry was taking my side, but I was on to him. I knew he just wanted to win me over for my mother. Still, I was willing to accept his defense.

My mother sighed. "He can pick you up, but I'll take you home. You're only fourteen, Sam. That's the best I can do." She had on her *I'm warning you* eyes. Perry winked at me.

"Mom, doesn't it hurt your face when you do that?" I said, making her laugh finally. Secretly I was thrilled, because I was actually going to the dance with Stone McLemore.

My mother wore her dumb black capri pants with loafers and a striped shirt while all the other mothers wore dresses cinched at the waist with belts to show off their figures. I wore a green skirt, and I parted my hair down the middle the way I'd seen Mary Alice do.

When he came to the door, the sound of my name in his voice took my breath away and made my legs shaky. I hated myself for feeling this way because it was so predictable and "girly." But still, I knew then what that expression "weak in the knees" meant. That was exactly how I felt. He was so handsome, I almost couldn't look at him face-to-face when he came over and pinned a flower to my sweater. Right then, right there, I knew this would be the most wonderful night of my life thus far.

I was grateful my mother didn't make a big deal out of questioning him or telling him what to do. We introduced him to Perry. They shook hands. We all left the house at the same time.

As Stone drove the three blocks to our school, I sat there in his car and admired the modern sweep of his dashboard.

"So tell me more about this Perry Walker," he said.

"I still can't figure out why you were there at the lunch counter downtown, making fun of that girl," I said. "How could you do that?"

"I wasn't making fun. I never said anything. I just watched. I didn't hurt anybody," he said. "I just happened to be there."

"So, you just stood there and watched?"

"That's what you were doing too."

We both went quiet. I hadn't thought of that.

"You're making too big a deal out of this, Samantha," he said. "Tonight's supposed to be fun, remember?"

"You're not one of them, are you? You're not like a member of the Klan or something, right?"

He sighed and shook his head.

"But why were you there?"

"It's against the law in Mississippi for blacks and whites to eat at the same counter—you know that," he said. "They broke the law, Samantha."

"Then maybe the law is wrong. Maybe that's what should be broken."

"How can you say that? If the law is wrong, then my parents are wrong and our teachers are wrong. How can you even say that?"

Then he pulled over by the side of the road. My heart was beating fast. "Look, Samantha." He wasn't angry. He spoke calmly, even softly then. "I'm just trying to figure all this out, just like everybody else, okay? You know what my mom's like.

And my dad. You've met them. I have to live with them." I nodded. I could understand that. Stone was older than I was, but he was still only sixteen. We both of us sighed then. I didn't want to argue and I didn't think Stone did either. It was strange to want to be with someone you didn't agree with.

Our school was lit up, and inside, the decorations committee had strung balloons and streamers from the gym ceiling and through the basketball hoops. Stone and I watched other people dance until we agreed we were thirsty and went for the punch bowl.

Soon enough some new song came on, and then there they were, Perry and my mother dancing in the middle of the gymnasium floor, with everyone making a circle around them, watching them, and all I could think was *This is no good at all.*

Stone and I stood in front of the punch table until he excused himself to talk with a group of his friends. I worried that I bored him. It seemed like Stone was someone who always needed people around him, orbiting him, his satellites other boys, mostly. I supposed I was mostly a loner, standing there like Pluto, sipping cherry-flavored punch. I looked for Ears but didn't see him.

Then I heard: "How come you don't dance like your mom?"

I heard: "Your mom is like a teenager. You're nothing like your mom."

I heard: "Is your mom a beatnik? My mom says she dresses like one."

I even overheard our principal, Mr. Calhoun, tell Miss Jenkins that my mother looked like a young Lesley Caron, the way she looked in that movie *Daddy Long Legs*.

When was this going to get fun? When was this going to become my night and not my mother's?

I sat down in a chair. When Elvis came on, my feet started tapping and I didn't think the chair would hold me, but that passed and another song started. I was beginning to think Stone had ditched me.

Patti Page was singing "Tennessee Waltz" when I finally heard Stone call *my* name, not my mother's.

I had never danced with a boy. I wondered if my face looked funny this way, looking up, and if my hair spread out over my shoulders the way it was supposed to. I wanted Stone to look the other way for a minute so I could reorganize myself.

He put one hand around my waist and he took my other hand and held it up steady in the air, and then we began to move. We didn't step on each other once. My chin just about reached his shoulder so that I could glance around to see if anyone saw us. But I didn't even care who saw, or what they were saying about my mother or Perry anymore. *I* was dancing and I was dancing with Stone McLemore. Even his ears were clean and fine-looking, and every now and then my lips brushed against his left lobe.

Was this love? Was this what my mother felt when she'd first danced with my dad?

Stone's shoulders felt man-like, and I wondered when that happened, when a boy's shoulders became man shoulders. Maybe when they began to read the paper in the morning and watched the TV news, maybe that's when shoulders changed. In movies I had seen girls talking while they danced, so I thought I should too. I told Stone what I'd heard my mother and Perry discussing. I told him about spies and stuff I didn't know anything about going on in Leningrad and Moscow. I thought what I said sounded secretive and romantic, especially whispered.

"You sure know a lot about Commies," he said, smiling, pulling me toward him. "Where'd you find all this out?"

"I watch. I listen," I said, looking into his eyes, then looking away, feeling like a spy. I couldn't hold my gaze for long because I thought my knees would give out. "Just like you do."

"Yeah, but who are you listening to?"

I nodded toward my mother dancing with Perry.

He pulled me closer.

Just then, it really did feel as though my whole body was made for him to hold.

My mother and Perry danced to "Fever" until someone turned it off because the lyrics and the way Peggy Lee said them were supposedly improper, which was good, because now maybe my mother and Perry would quit dancing.

We had all agreed to leave from the school. Stone offered Perry a ride back home, and we all laughed or tried to laugh at the strange arrangement. I was to leave with my mother even though Stone offered again to drive me home.

"That was the agreement, remember?" she said in the parking lot. "Sam, I'll be over here by the car."

Stone faced me and put both his hands on my shoulders. "I had a great time, Samantha."

"Me too," I said.

We started to lean in to kiss.

"Sam!" my mother called.

My mother and I drove back home in her old beige VW Bug, our faces filling with light from time to time as a car passed from the opposite direction. My mother's car was littered with lecture notes, books, empty coffee cups, and stray pencils and pens, and it still smelled of the suntan lotion I spilled on the floor last summer.

"I haven't danced since, well, since your father was alive," she said.

"He's not your boyfriend," I said. "Perry can't be your boyfriend."

I waited, but she didn't say anything. And that's when I knew. He *was* her boyfriend, and I wanted to throw up.

She turned on the car radio. She liked the new song playing, and she turned it up. *"Louie Louie,"* she sang. *"Aww. We gotta go now."*

We heard the sirens first. Then came the flashing lights.

"Stay calm," my mother said, looking in the rearview mirror, slowing down, and then pulling over to the side of the road. "I'll handle this." She turned off the radio. My mother hadn't done anything wrong driving that I could tell. She was a good driver. My grandmother was the bad driver in the family, but she never got stopped because everybody in the state seemed to know her.

"Evening, miss," the officer said. "You know how fast you were going?"

"I'm not sure."

"You were going forty in a fifty-mile-an-hour zone. You were going under the speed limit, which is just as serious as going over."

My mother and I looked at each other.

"I'm so sorry," my mother said. Her voice sounded shaky. Just that week we had heard that two black men had been arrested for no cause, then taken to the basement of the police station and beaten.

"We've just come from my daughter's high school dance."

The officer shined his flashlight in my face, then he moved the light all over us.

"You look like a nice lady," he said then to my mother. "How come you're wearing those clothes?"

I think we thought he was kidding. The question startled us so that we both said "Ha" without knowing or thinking about what we had just done. And it was the worst possible thing we could have done. We laughed. And then we laughed not once, but twice.

We both realized exactly what we had done when we saw the policeman's face. My mother gripped the steering wheel and froze. He reached in and took her car keys, then opened the door and took her by the arm. I held on to her other arm. We were both pulling, while she had hold of the steering wheel.

"Miss. You're under arrest."

"For what?"

"Tell your girl to let go."

"Let go, Sam," she said. "I'm all right. We're all right. This is a nice police officer. He's a gentleman. He's not here to do us harm." She was saying these things to convince herself or the policeman, not me. I saw that her hands were shaking.

"Mom?"

Already he had taken her out of the car. He was handcuffing my mother, while she leaned against the car.

"What about my daughter?"

He looked in, and it was like he was just remembering me again. He sighed. We waited. I thought I heard the sound of a few cicadas hanging on to summer, humming. My ears were full up with humming and ringing, leftover noise from the dance. I wasn't sure if I was still breathing.

Then, just as quickly as he had cuffed her, the officer uncuffed my mother.

"Consider this a warning," he said.

We drove home in silence. Even though the night air was warm, we couldn't stop shaking.

"Mom," I said after a while. "Aren't you going to report this?"

"Report it? Report it to whom? The police?"

That night the house seemed suddenly too big. It had too many windows and dark corners. My mother turned on every light, then turned them all off again. She locked and bolted all the doors and we sat together on the sofa, watching, waiting—for what, we weren't sure. Then, when we grew sleepy, I didn't hesitate to climb into her big bed and she didn't stop me.

CHAPTER 7

STONE CALLED ME THE NEXT MORNING. He said he was sorry our big evening had been cut short and he had wanted so badly to drive me home. We both knew what that meant. It meant we could have kissed again. He was wondering if my mother would allow him to take me out that night to look at the stars. I wasn't used to talking with a boy on the phone. I thought of Stone standing in the McLemore kitchen, or sitting in his room. The McLemores even had phones that didn't have a dial, but buttons with numbers you pushed. I put down the receiver and ran to my mother's room to ask.

She hesitated, but after I begged and begged, my mother said that I could go out with Stone, only for a little while. She had lectures to go over and papers to grade. She sat at her desk with open books all around her and a blank sheet of paper already in the typewriter, daring her. She was behind with everything and I could tell she just wanted me to leave her alone.

We went through some nearby woods, then hiked up to the top of an old Indian mound that had escaped being subdivided. There was a full moon and the sky was clear and bright. The night was still, and the stars were all over the place. Stone brought a telescope and we took turns looking through it.

He knew so much. He told me that Ptolemy of Alexandria developed the idea of the sun and planets moving around the earth in the second century. He told me someone in the thirteenth century figured out that a tube filled with gunpowder and lit at one end gave a push as the gasses rushed out, and boom, you've got a rocket. Stone knew about guns and bombs and where the Milky Way was. But then we turned our focus on the moon. I felt the way Galileo must have felt looking at the moon for the first time through *his* telescope, seeing the lunar surface clearly marked by craters. It wasn't perfect. The moon wasn't perfect and there wasn't a man *in* it, but Stone and I both knew that soon there might be a man *on* it.

Stone built a little fire and we roasted marshmallows. He was an Eagle Scout, so he knew about camping, being outside, and the maps of the moon marked with sections of seas called Ocean of Storms, Sea of Clouds, Sea of Serenity, and the Sea of Tranquility, where the first astronauts were headed. The fire illuminated his smile. Goose bumps ran over my scalp. We grew quiet.

"I'm sorry that your dad died," he said after a while. "My parents can drive me crazy, but. Well. That must be hard for you and your mom."

"I miss him." I thought about that. "I really do."

"What was he like?"

"He was handsome and fun. He was always game to do stuff, you know? He liked to read but he wasn't at all like my mom. He was good in science." We smiled at each other then, Stone and I. Maybe because we both realized that when I described my dad, I was also describing Stone.

We lay down together on top of fallen pine needles, staring at the sky. His jacket smelled of wood smoke. We stared at the moon until a blue ring appeared. "Try this," he said. "Let yourself relax, and focus on the space between the moon and the stars. Don't think about anything. Then let yourself float. If you can, you can ride up there with them."

We went quiet and we stayed quiet together in a way that felt like we were talking.

Then after a while, he said, "My dad says they're trying to destroy Christianity and democracy and change what Mississippi's all about."

"Who's 'they'?" I wished he could just keep talking about the moon.

"The Kennedys. Outsiders."

"I don't understand why you'd hate President Kennedy," I said, making my voice go soft. "He's the one who's behind your space age. He's the one getting us to the moon."

"Someday we'll move on to other planets; the moon is just a training ground." His voice sounded calm now, especially as he began to go on and tell me about the combustion process, fuel functions, oxidizers, compressed gas, and thrust. He rolled over and turned toward me then, holding my face between his hands.

"I love knowing that I'm keeping you safe, Samantha Thomas." He drew me so close that I could almost taste the sweet marshmallow of his breath. "Don't you like knowing that too?"

It was such a strange question, I couldn't take it seriously. "*Nyet,*" I said with a put-on Russian accent. He squeezed my jaw with his hand.

"Sometimes you're too smart for your own good." He

brought my mouth up to his and we kissed and kissed, hard until we went gentle.

I couldn't help but feel like my world was coming out of focus, and it wasn't a bad feeling at all. Everything was moving and changing—the clouds, the moon, the earth, our town, us, me.

Anything could have happened there in those woods. Anything magical and anything evil too.

My mother was on the phone with my grandmother when I got back home that night. Stone was careful not to keep me out late. He said he wanted to earn my mother's respect. When he told me this, I liked him even more.

My mother held the phone almost at arm's length and I could hear my grandmother's voice.

"I want you both here right now. I want you out of that town. I want you to sleep here under this roof. You are no longer safe there. You need to be with your own people." My grandmother claimed to know more than most about violence in Mississippi because her mother, father and aunt lived during the Civil War and had told her everything she knew. Even though my great-aunt's name was Little Bit, she was considered a strong woman, one of the toughest ladies, and she lived to be ninety-five years old. My grandmother's name was Thelma Addy. Most people knew her for her bridge playing, her good housekeeping, and her fruit preserves.

I waited for them to get off the phone. I wanted to tell my mother about Stone. I wanted to ask her questions about these strange new feelings I had.

My mother bit her lower lip. "I appreciate the offer— really, I do." She was still formal with my dad's mother. "But I'm afraid we can't come for Thanksgiving. I'm giving this party, and I just can't cancel. I'm up for promotion, you know."

My mother had already invited students and faculty over for Thanksgiving in two days' time—all the people who didn't go home over the short holiday. The left-behinds, that's what Perry called them.

"Maybe we can come for Sam's birthday," she said. I don't know why she didn't just say Christmas, because I had been cursed with a Christmas birthday.

Willa Mae stayed with us the day before Thanksgiving and we made a champagne punch and boiled five pounds of Gulf Coast shrimp the following day because my mother hated turkey. All afternoon Perry, Willa Mae, and I used shot glasses to make circles out of slices of expensive Pepperidge Farm bread, the kind we used only for company and never for lunch sandwiches. He talked to me about taking pictures.

"You can't be afraid of your subject," he said. "You're be-hind the camera and it's like your shield, your armor. Nothing can hurt you when you've got proof." He picked up one of the little white bread rounds and held it up like a shield. I did the same and we played at jousting.

We made mounds of bread rounds, and Willa Mae wouldn't let us throw out the crusts. She put them in bags to freeze for the day she would make some of her good bread pudding. Then we spread the bread rounds with butter and carefully laid cucumber slices on top or dabbed them with black and red caviar from a jar.

After a while Willa Mae and I told the story again about what had happened that day at the drugstore. It made us both shake to talk about it, but we still wanted to tell the story again.

"And all because they didn't want those students sitting at the lunch counter," I said.

"Aha!" Perry said. "An agitator in the making!"

"There are a lot of rules in this world—good ones and not-so-good ones," my mother said. "You still gotta follow them all or work with the system to change them. That's what living in our country is all about."

I rolled my eyes. "Mom. Sometimes you can sound like such a teacher-mom."

Willa Mae laughed and shook her head and told me I was walking on thin ice.

My mother decided to make the party a celebration of the college's new art acquisition: an all-red canvas painting the school had just purchased from an artist who also blew up balloons and sold them, calling them artworks of his breath.

My mother didn't like this artist's work, but she said hosting a party would hopefully let her win back points with members of the tenure and promotion committee. She said people were still whispering about her "mistake" at Tougaloo.

The leaves hadn't all fallen and you still didn't need a coat. Next door our neighbors gathered and took pictures of one another dressed up, because they were celebrating Thanksgiving like every other normal family in Jackson. They stood in their new clothes in front of their house. I wanted to shout out to them to focus, to stand in the light, or not stand out at all because they looked too staged and tense. None of them knew what to do with their hands.

The students who came from my mother's college looked shaggy. The girls wore short skirts and black stockings or narrow slacks, no lipstick, lots of powder, and heavy eye makeup. Perry told me they were dressing like actresses they'd seen in New Wave films. Perry had his Pentax camera around his neck, focused, he said, from two feet to infinity.

One boy held his packet of Old Golds while he blew cigarette smoke, talking to a girl he was trying to impress. He was saying, "Need is an autoinduced mechanism implanted by the corporate culture that unfortunately permeates our innermost thoughts." I stepped away from them and laughed when Perry rolled his eyes.

Our house grew crowded with students and professors all eating and talking at once about "cultural space" and "interiority." Did they make these words up? Cultural space—what was that supposed to mean?

I heard one student ask one of the professors if he thought white people were better than black people. The professor looked at the student and said, "Son, we stopped talking about that when Darwin settled the matter. We're all people. We're just going to have to live with that."

Perry had taken out his camera and was snapping pictures of everyone talking.

"Couldn't you work some magic and make me look prettier?" my mother said. She kept moving her face to the right because she didn't like pictures showing her right side. "Take some pounds off here?" she said, laughing, putting her hands on her hips. "Use a soft-focus filter or something?" She smiled as she said this.

He told my mother to look out the window and she did, and I could see what he saw. I could see her face lit up. I could see her beauty.

I was glad then that he didn't say anything dinky like, "Oh, you are so beautiful, you need no enhancing." He didn't say anything at all. He never took his right eye away from his camera. He kept clicking and clicking, moving around the room. My mother looked so happy.

Watching Perry work, I saw that he became serious and focused so that the rest of us might as well have all fallen away. He was there, but he was not there. He sweated. He moved differently and as easily as a cat. My mother had told me Perry hated teaching, but that he was among the best.

"Photography's not art," I heard someone telling Perry. "Art shouldn't have anything to do with mechanical equipment or technology. It should be an artist and a pen, a paintbrush, or some clay."

"You obviously haven't seen Perry's photographs," my mother said. My mother wore a new sleeveless shift made out of material that said *Fragile: Handle with Care* all over it. Perry had gotten her this dress from some new shop. On her arm she wore a silver cuff that looked as though it could take bullets. Her black hair was still short, but it looked tangled and somehow undone. She pushed her foot back and forth in her shoe as she stood and talked.

Everyone was talking at once about art. They used words such as *banal, Dadaist aesthetic value,* and *intrinsic.* I watched my mother's face. She pretended to be okay with modern art, but I knew she really loved Rubens and Rembrandt, Renoir and Degas. She loved the landscapes by Poussin, the still lifes of

Caravaggio, and all those cloudy paintings by Monet. All she wanted to do was see a van Gogh or any other European painting up close, then go to Thessaly and Greece and see the theaters of Pergamum and of Epidaurus, where, she told me, poppies grew nearby.

School was different in college. These teachers and students *argued*. They were still asking questions. They talked about ethics and consequences. They knew details along with facts. They knew about big things like wars but they also knew about little things like how Mussolini's army poured acid on the desert sands when barefooted Ethiopian soldiers chased them down in Abyssinia.

Later, after all the eating, I found Perry outside, humming some song, swinging on the rope swing the previous owner had left behind hanging from a black walnut tree in our backyard. His cigarette was burned down nearly to his fingertips while he sat there, his camera slung over and around his neck, resting on his back.

"If you're so good at what you do, why are you here?" I asked.

"That's some attitude. Good things can come to the most unlikely places, you know. I'm a good guy, Sam." He looked at me. "Seriously." He stomped out his cigarette and looked up at the sky. "Once upon a time I took a picture of a soldier shooting Korean prisoners in the back. Their hands were tied, their legs bound. They'd photographed executions before; usually they were out-of-focus shots because the photographer flinched. This was a good, clear image. My editor at *Life* took one look at the picture and he said, 'American soldiers don't shoot people in the back.' So that was that."

"You quit?"

He shook his head. "I was fired."

I went quiet. I'd never known anyone who had actually gotten fired. It felt a little like talking to someone who'd been in prison. "My mom could get fired too, you know."

He nodded. "You know, at *Life* we used to outline our assignments. I couldn't outline all that's happening here, though. You can't make this up," he said. "Who knows? Maybe this was the way it was supposed to be. Maybe I was meant to come back from the war to take pictures of the one going on down here."

This time I didn't say, *What war?* This time I knew what he was talking about.

"I don't know. There are some things about the South I guess I just don't get," he went on. "A maid gets fifteen cents an hour cooking, laundering, ironing, mopping, sweeping, changing the sheets, and everybody expects her to be grateful."

I thought about that. I thought about Willa Mae and all the men outside the drugstore, billy-clubbing those women. "I know Willa Mae gets more than fifteen cents an hour."

Perry smiled. "Come on," he said, getting out of the swing and taking my hand. "We can't change the world tonight. Let's go back inside and tell these pointy-headed intellectuals and pretentious students a thing or two."

Inside, while I went around with a garbage sack and cleared paper plates, students started to recite their poetry without any complete sentences. One said things like "All that's left is." And "Untranslatable." Another made different vowel sounds, clicking out a tune with his tongue, a kind of song without words, both beautiful and annoying. I didn't want to like it, but I couldn't help but listen.

Perry was talking to a man in the corner of the room. "We need someone to take pictures," he said to Perry. "If we don't get the pictures, they'll act like it never happened." Perry was nodding, repeating the time and day. "It's the only time they have off to register to vote."

Perry nodded, and said, "Okay, okay. I'll be there."

Someone was reciting a poem about tangerines and misery, ending with the line "chew, swallow, made into flesh and the imagination of our lives to come, amen." Everyone clapped. Some snapped their fingers.

I fell asleep in my mother's room next to the pile of everybody's coats spread out on her bed. I woke up to the sound of Perry's voice, "Why are you here?"

He wasn't talking to me. He was in the next room somewhere with my mother. All the coats were gone. Everyone had left, so I could hear Perry clearly. He said, "You weren't even born here. Your husband was."

"This is the closest thing to home and family I have," my mother said.

"You know, when I came here, I gave this place a few months. One year max," Perry said. "But now? Now is different. I wanna stay and I wanna stay here with you and Sam. This is my place. You're my home."

"All I'm asking, Perry, is that you not go," my mother said. "Let someone else do it this time. It's getting too dangerous."

"They're registering to vote, honey. The timing couldn't be better. They need someone with a camera. No one else'll go. If you want, you can go too. You could help register."

"I can't get involved, you know that. My job's already in jeopardy. I have Samantha to think of."

I crept up out of the bed and tiptoed to the doorway.

Perry was leaning in to my mother as he listened to what she said. They talked so close. He only leaned closer, his hands on the table, his leg touching hers.

"It's so risky," my mother said. "*Why* are you doing this?"

"Because I'm a human being. Because we're all human beings."

My mother closed her eyes and winced. Maybe her hearing aid was ringing and bothering her, but as I watched her turn down the volume, I wanted to tell her right then that she couldn't quiet *all* those outside voices forever.

"Come with me," he said. "I'll take care of you and Samantha. I promise." They kissed lightly, both of them leaning in. It was more hug than kiss, more meaning than anything else. My mother smiled when they broke away. This man made her happy. Maybe she was thinking what I was thinking too. Why did the men in our lives head for danger, all for the sake of doing the right thing? They kissed nothing like the way Stone and I kissed, and I wished then more than anything that at some point in my life I would get kissed that way.

CHAPTER 8

FOR OUR STATE REPORT, everyone else in my class cut out pictures from magazines and newspapers, neatly marking them *This is a picture of . . .* and then saying what it was a picture of. Mary Alice had always received high marks in handwriting, and she signed her name in perfect Palmer script. The words I wrote came out looking spidery.

Mary Alice hung up maps we recognized from her family's air-raid shelter. She had also dressed up her dolls to look like early settlers. Ken stood inside a hexagonal hatbox decorated to resemble an early log cabin. Two of her Barbies wore big hoop skirts with crinoline to look like southern belles. They lingered together in another hatbox made to look like Tara from *Gone With the Wind*.

Mary Alice's hair was pulled back into a soft, shiny ponytail. She was arranging the Spanish moss on top of the hatboxes when I came into the classroom to set up my report.

I didn't have any dressed-up dolls. I just had the pictures I had taken with Perry Walker's camera, pictures I had taken during my walks around our neighborhood, and pictures I had taken when Perry took us for those long car rides. I had a picture of Willa Mae holding a packet of snuff in her apron in front of a row of hollyhocks and Confederate jasmine. I had a picture of a bottle tree and a family of ducks crossing a street. I had pictures of Willa Mae picking up the garbage in our yard and my mother scrubbing off the words WE ARE WATCHING from our front door. I had a picture of the police officer standing outside the drugstore while an angry man billy-clubbed a black woman. I had an underexposed picture of football players, silhouetted, hunched down, ready to charge each other. I had a picture of an old white man fishing while beyond him a church finishes burning. I had a picture of the inside of an empty sharecropper's house with calendars of the past the only decoration in the room. I had a picture of the big magnolia in our front yard—a close-up of a blossom past its prime, in the first stages of turning brown. I had taped them all to some posterboard.

There was a written report too, meant to go along with the presentation.

All day I thought over the written report I handed in. I had proofread it, then retyped it using my mother's black Underwood, the G coming out smudgy and looking a lot like an O. My mother asked if I needed any help, but I didn't want my mother messing with it. This was all my work, all mine. I was going for articulate and well organized. Those were the main criteria my mother used when she graded papers. But I was also after compelling, which I knew would bump the paper somewhere into the A zone. I covered everything: the state's symbols, including a picture of its coat of arms and motto: *The committee to design a coat of arms was appointed by legislative action February 7, 1894, and the design proposed by that committee was accepted and became the official coat of arms.*

When she finally got to my setup, Miss Jenkins looked and looked and then stared at the browning magnolia. All she said finally was that it was a shame I couldn't find a better flower—one fresher and more representative of the beautiful magnolia that was our state flower.

She glanced at the pictures a second time, her face looking like she was being forced to eat a bowl of lemons. She told me my captions were difficult to read and therefore "inadequate." She said I left out the state bird even though I told her I'd tried but the mockingbird wouldn't sit still long enough for me to photograph it.

Ears brought in his jar of cicadas. They had sidetracked him altogether, and his report turned into a report about cicadas. He found out all kinds of interesting facts, like that cicadas were the only insects to have developed such an effective and specialized means of producing sound. Some species produced a noise intensity that approached the pain threshold of the human ear. Other species have songs so high in pitch that the noise was beyond the range of our hearing. Ears even brought in the Bible, which he turned open to the Book of Revelation, that part about a swarm of locusts with scorpion tails and human faces that torments the unbelievers.

We watched Miss Jenkins's strange smile as she looked over Ears's work. "I see that you became quite interested in our plague this summer, Ears," she said. "The problem here is that the cicada has nothing to do with Mississippi. It's neither the state bug nor the state bird."

Some people laughed when she said this. I knew that she was going to give Ears an F or make him do it all over.

"I thought your report was real interesting," I whispered to Ears.

He shrugged.

When Mary Alice asked about our grades, Miss Jenkins told the class that our state report grades would come in the mail along with our final grades at Christmas.

At lunch Ears shared food his mother had packed for the two of us, and we feasted on saltines and a can of sardines and Vienna sausages each. For dessert we split the one Moon Pie. Then Mary Alice and her friends busted up our fun wanting to play a game that involved tying Ears to the magnolia tree so that they could circle around him like they were in some powwow, but Ears and I would have none of it.

The sun had come out and it wouldn't quit. Mary Alice had her right hand above her eyes. "What are you telling me?"

I looked at Mary Alice standing there with her little gang of look-alikes. I didn't want to be like them or think like them to fit in anymore. "Me? I'm telling you you're acting like you're still in third grade," I said, staring her down till someone else said something about letting us losers be by ourselves.

"What's your real name anyway?" I asked Ears after they had all gone away. "I'm sick of calling you Ears."

"Tempe," he said. "After my great-granddaddy."

On the last day of school before Christmas break, we spent the day spray-painting pinecones silver and gold for wreaths we made to take home to our parents as gifts, and at the end of the day we all sang the state song, which we had memorized.

"Go, Mississippi, keep rolling along," we sang, saying "Mizippi" for Mississippi. "Go, Mississippi, you cannot go wrong."

When school was out, Stone stood outside our classroom and walked me to my locker. I was so surprised that I couldn't think of anything to say. Ever since the dance, Stone had kept his distance from me while we were at school. People didn't even know we knew each other or liked each other. I don't even think Mary Alice knew. I wanted other people to see me talking to Stone. I wanted them to look at me and think, My, my. Look at that Samantha Thomas. She's no loser. She might just be okay. She might even be a little bit interesting. I couldn't help but notice that Stone and I were most together when we were alone. When we were with other people, we were apart. And we were most of the time with other people. I wondered if he was ashamed to be seen with me. Or was this the way things were with boys and girls? If that was so, I wanted us to be different. I wanted our separateness to change. I opened my locker to gather my books.

"I got you a Christmas present," he said. He gave me a small wrapped box. "Open it."

"But I didn't get you anything," I said.

"That's not the way it works," he said. "Open it."

Inside was a necklace with a gold cross pendant.

"Here," he said, picking the necklace out of the box. "Let me."

I turned around, then lifted my hair off my neck. He hooked the necklace. People watched. The bell rang. I turned around.

"You look so pretty." Stone looked at me then, smiled, and took my hand. Stone was holding my hand, right there in school!

"Do you have any plans for the holidays?" he asked.

"We're going to my grandparents'," I said. "But I want to do something . . . I don't know . . . special. Significant."

He laughed. "Does it involve me?"

I shrugged and smiled. "I'm not sure you'd understand."

"Try me."

I thought only briefly of that old saying "Loose lips sink ships." My grandmother had told me about that silly saying they'd used during World War I to keep people from talking about where the soldiers were stationed.

"It's something Perry's involved in, helping folks register to vote. I want to help too. So maybe my mom and I will."

Stone's smile dropped into a frown. He let go of my hand. "You should stay out of that, Samantha. Really. That's not business of yours."

"What are you talking about? It's all our business. You saw what happened at the drugstore, right? You were there."

"I'm not talking about this with you, Samantha. You don't know what you're saying. It's dangerous."

"You sound like my mother."

"She only wants what's best for you."

"What's best for me isn't always so important." Some people looked up. I was startled by my own voice. I slammed my locker door shut, turned, and headed home.

CHAPTER 9

On Christmas Eve, our house shook us awake. We heard a crash and then a car skidding off. My mother and I both dropped from our beds to the floor. We had read and heard about Molotov cocktails—homemade bombs made with gasoline in a bottle and a rag pushed down in it for a wick. At night, white boys or men in cars lit the rag and tossed these home-made bombs into yards throughout Jackson. I crawled across my room and peeked out the window. Our lawn wasn't on fire. Somebody had thrown the bomb into the yard of a preacher who lived right behind us. The previous Sunday he had been preaching for desegregation in his church. My mother came to my room and called for me to get back down and away from the windows. We huddled together on the floor in the hallway.

"You used to tell me to sing when I was scared, remember?" I said.

"So sing, then."

"The farmer in the dell," I started. *"The farmer in the dell. Hi-ho, the derry-o, the farmer in the dell.* That's all I know."

"The farmer takes a wife," she said, not singing. "And then: The wife takes a child."

There on the floor, my mother put her arm over my back while we tried to sing "The Farmer in the Dell" every now and then. We stayed down on the floor like that, listening for more noise or voices or both, until we both finally fell asleep.

My mother turned off the car. It was Christmas Day and my birthday too. The night before I was fourteen, but that morning I turned fifteen. For me, gifts weren't more plentiful on a Christmas birthday, but some years the presents were a little bit better than other years.

We could hear nothing but the crickets my grandfather kept in his carport for fishing bait. They wouldn't quit. An hour away from where we lived, the air smelled clean and piney here in Franklin.

"They're not always very pleasant to listen to, are they?"

my mother said, flipping down the sun visor to look in the mirror. "Ready?"

"Perry could be here," I said. "You invited him, right?"

"He had too much work. And besides, it would be awkward."

"He's a good guy, Mom. You're the one who used to tell me to go with your gut."

"I invited him! He had too much work."

"We should have dragged him along."

My grandmother stood inside the door and waved us in, then, growing impatient, she came hurrying out of the house.

"Maybe you and I both need some time away," my mother said, putting on lipstick.

"From Perry?"

"From everything. From Jackson."

My mother and I were both tired from the night before.

My mother asked me not to tell my grandparents or my cousins about anything. She didn't want anyone worrying. More than anything, I think my mother wanted to get away from nights like the one we'd just had.

My grandmother came up to the car. She opened the car door and we hugged. She smelled of perfume and Listerine both. "You're too old for this," she told me, straightening my white shirt with the Peter Pan collar. "You need a proper dress." I told her what I figured she wanted to hear: that school was great, that I had a lot of new friends, that my mother was a shoo-in for her promotion.

Then she turned to my mother, taking her by the shoulders, standing back and looking her up and down. My mother wore a gray dress and white socks and loafers like she had worn way back when she went to graduate school. The brown leather was scuffed and they still bore the pennies my father had put in before he left for the war.

"Martha. You should wear something else besides gray. You're too pretty for dull colors."

"I find gray a very comforting color," my mother said.

"Honey. It's hardly a color at all. You'll never meet a man wearing that."

My mother shook her head, smiling.

"You look exhausted." My grandmother would make my mother cocklebur tea, which she said cured everything. "How are you ever going to meet anyone looking so exhausted?"

"What other mother-in-law wants her daughter-in-law to meet a man?"

My grandmother didn't even hesitate. "Naomi wants her daughter-in-law Ruth to remarry. In the Bible. Naomi's the one who tells Ruth how to nab Boaz."

"Maybe I *have* met someone already," my mother said.

"Oh?" my grandmother said, looking back and forth between my mother and me.

As we all went in, I made smoochy-smoochy sounds until my mother pleaded for me to stop.

My grandmother wore her red Christmas dress and black, hard, low-heeled shoes that clicked across the hallway floor as she led us inside.

My dad was born and raised in Franklin, Mississippi, a town off the highway that Ulysses S. Grant himself said was too beautiful to burn. My grandparents still lived right outside Franklin, out past the counties with the forgotten Indian names.

They lived on a house built on Choctaw land. My grandmother told me the Choctaw had been here first, long before white people. Locals claimed they heard their ghostly shouts and wails on stormy winter nights. There was barely any trace left of the Indians in Mississippi except for the names of so many rivers and towns, which I liked saying more than anything, names that felt so good zzzing around in my mouth—Yazoo, Tallahatchie, Bogue Chitoe.

My father told me once he had loved living in Franklin but he hadn't cared for his chores. Once, while he showed me how to feed the chickens, he told me that they were terrible birds. He said that when they smelled the blood of another injured bird they would surround it and peck it to death.

My grandparents' house was altogether different from our house in Jackson. My mother, who preferred wearing black and gray clothes, also liked a black and gray house. Inside my grandparents' old Victorian house, paintings of tulips and roses and watercolor magnolias hung on the walls next to portraits of our ancestors. At our house in Jackson, my mother hung only framed posters of European oil paintings, bought at art shows. No family pictures, not even of us.

It was mayhem inside my grandparents' house on Christmas when we all came together for the day. First and second cousins came running to greet us, making the china and crystal in my grandmother's china cabinet rattle and chime. My mother lowered the volume on her hearing aid.

Everything looked so old and falling-apart at my grandparents' house. Compared to the McLemores' bright, clean home, everything here in Franklin looked dirty and crumbly. The walls were a dull yellow, the color of cooked squash, and the glossy paint peeled from all the ceilings. The county water was hard, and all that sulfur made rings in the white sinks. It was terrible to use the bathroom, because now I saw the yellow ring around the tub. Only the summer before I hadn't even noticed.

Aunt Ida came and went, slamming doors, picking fights with her oldest. She was good at that. Aunt Ida was married to my father's brother Ted.

Uncle Ted had gone away to an Ivy League college in the East, where he got drunk his senior year and rode a horse into the administration building and up and down the stairs, allowing it to "desecrate" the marble halls. He was kicked out before graduation, and when he came home he was given a job in town at the bank, taking people's money, lending people money, and telling funny college stories over and over at Thanksgiving and Christmas. Never mind that he never graduated or got the degree.

My grandfather waved to us while reciting Robert Burns poetry and passages from the Rubaiyat as he did a slow crawl across the swimming pool. Nobody was outside listening, so I went out to be polite. He clung to the ladder of the pool, switching to that story about driving the ice truck to the Neshoba County Fair one year. My grandfather had studied law and had his own practice in Franklin for years until he retired only recently.

"You have a good swim?" I asked him when he came out of the pool.

"Oh, yeah," he said, not even smiling. "I got wet."

He put a towel around himself and hugged me. Then my grandfather, who was mostly annoyed that so many people were in his house, disappeared into his bedroom and slept until someone called him in for supper.

We waited for everyone to arrive before we opened presents. Another batch of cousins drove up in a paneled station wagon, its back end scraping the concrete as they pulled into the drive. They were still singing some road song as they all piled out, brushing their hair, putting stuff on their eyelids, and carrying purses they didn't even need.

My mother grew quiet whenever she visited Franklin. Maybe it was because there was so much noise there. Or maybe she didn't say much because my grandmother, without saying very much herself, seemed to have everything under control—the food, the house, the family. Even though my mother and my grandmother didn't get along all the time, they were a lot alike.

It was so loud when we all came together in that house. All those voices just made me want to climb into myself. I couldn't get outside fast enough to join the pack of cousins listening to the radio out on the porch.

Aunt Ida wouldn't let us listen to the new Elvis. She was still seething over Elvis doing a slow bump and grind on national TV at the end of "Hound Dog" on *The Milton Berle Show* a gazillion years ago. She said Elvis's obscene and offensive gyrating was an outrage and could only lead to teenage delinquency.

There were seven of us cousins who lived nearby now. I was no longer considered a 100 percent Yankee. It was more like 40 percent now. We only had one cousin who was a full-fledged Yankee, an older boy who we once saw swing a cat in circles by its tail. His mother was my father's sister Irene, named after my grandmother's mother. She had married a man up in Chicago. We hardly ever saw Aunt Irene.

"George Wallace has it right," Aunt Ida said. "Integration is gonna ruin this country."

I looked up and saw my mother turn her hearing aid completely off.

"He's a *noted* lawyer," Aunt Ida said of some relative living in Tupelo.

"A noted lawyer," my grandmother said, laughing, coming out with boiled shrimp. "Oh, for goodness' sake. What's gotten into this family? You'd think we'd dropped from heaven itself instead of working this land with our bare hands."

Us cousins grew bored with all the talk, and while my grandmother cooked in the kitchen and the rest of the grownups sat and talked about world politics, we set out to play capture-the-flag. I overheard my mother on the front porch gushing about the United Nations—how hopeful it was, how tolerant we all would become.

We played out back where my grandmother kept her kitchen garden. They grew all their own vegetables and herbs, and here and there were still eggplant, basil, hollyhocks, tomatoes, sweet potatoes, all kinds of greens, and clumps of crepe myrtle leading to the family cemetery. This is where my great-grandfather and great-grandmother Frank and Irene Russell lay buried. They died a week apart when they were both in their eighties. They lay next to the oldest grave, which belonged to my great-great-great-grandmother who died in the winter of 1862, the very same day my great-aunt Little Bit was born. Great-Aunt Little Bit was birthed by a Union soldier and swaddled in his Union shirt. That was a good story my grandmother told. Next to her lay my great-uncle Jack and their parents.

My grandmother, Thelma Addy, often told stories about her father, Frank Russell. Sometimes it felt like it might as well have been 1862 and not 1962. Sometimes, though, my grandmother told us about her own raising. She was born while the whole South was still trying to recover from the Civil War, and she told stories of a place called No-Bob, where a woman named Addy O'Donnell grew up and then went on to save my grandmother's life by curing her of thrush when she was a baby.

We had been farmers. That much was clear. Now we were lawyers, bankers, teachers, and housewives. Everybody here was supposed to know exactly where he or she came from, and we were to make sure that others knew it as well. Anybody else from any other family? Most likely, they'd come in on the *second* landing in 1742, whereas we had come in on the *first*.

We passed our hands through my grandmother's herbs, rubbing the rosemary and mint with our fingertips, knowing we would still have the smell on our hands late into the night. Some of the older cousins walked out into the woods to fish in our grandparents' pond. The woods bordered the black section of town, which Sherman had given to the newly freed slaves one hundred years ago.

I could hear the grownup voices still talking, coming through the screen door, sounding like a low, ongoing, cicada-like hum.

We captured the flag and went on to play war. None of us was too old for war. In fact, we older cousins made our pinecone artillery more powerful, more grenade-like, because we knew how exactly to pretend to bite off the top before throwing, and we knew how to mimic the sounds of explosions. I thought of my dad during our war games. I felt I became my dad. All of us grew up hearing stories about war and warring. Soldiers kept their mouths open when they fired off their cannons and guns, to release the pressure. Still, most of them lost their hearing anyway. We never grew tired of this game, and sometimes we quietly dared each other to make the fighting ever more real.

The youngest cousins ran scared back to the porch, where the grownups all sat on rockers, drinking and eating boiled peanuts. There they stayed on their mama's lap or else they took turns hand-churning the ice cream, adding the crushed peppermint sticks near the end.

Aunt Ida stood and said she was putting a stop to all our violent play. Each and every one of us would just have to quit. My grandmother told us to come to the porch for shrimp.

We all gathered around a white table set up with Gulf shrimp on ice, shrimp that we peeled and dipped in a cocktail sauce made with ketchup, lemon juice, and horseradish.

Aunt Ida wanted someone to snap a picture of all the grownups, and my mother offered up my services, saying I'd become a "pretty darn good photographer." She told me to get my camera, and even though I had sworn off taking pictures since my state report, I did what I was told. I still hadn't gotten my grade in the mail, but I kept thinking of Miss Jenkins's face when she saw my photographs.

They draped themselves over the porch rail, then turned to face me. Aunt Ida didn't know that the shade from a tree darkened half her face and the light only hit her reddened lips. Uncle Ted didn't know that his hairpiece was crooked. I centered the picture on my grandmother because it seemed the right thing to do.

"Say gumbo," I said.

I snapped the picture and they relaxed, happy now to be done with me, while Aunt Ida asked my mother where I got "gumbo." That's when I snapped another picture, the better picture.

"Christmas is more better than birthdays because you get more presents," my cousin Tine said, sitting cross-legged under the Christmas tree in the living room. She wasn't drooling or slurring her words as much as the year before. "The colors are prettier than they are in October too. I like red and green. I don't like orange or brown."

Already it was getting cold. My grandmother turned on the space heater and I could smell its woolly heat.

Everybody tore into presents we had all carefully wrapped and placed under the tree. This I never understood. It all seemed like such a waste. They oohed and ahhed over a gift only to put it aside to open another and another and another. My mother sat with my grandmother on the horsehair loveseat, watching.

"Why don't you and Samantha come here and live with us?" I heard my grandmother say quietly to my mother. "She can go to school here, and I'm sure we could find you a job at the junior college. It's getting so dangerous in Jackson. You need to be closer to family." After my father died, everyone in the family had urged my mother to live in Jackson because it was a city and there were more opportunities for modern, educated women like her. Now they were asking her to come back even closer.

I tried to imagine what our life would be like in Franklin, living in the same town with my grandparents. We would finally have the garden I wanted as my own, with pole beans, okra, and corn. My grandmother would needlepoint, a thimble on her first finger, quizzing me on *Pilgrim's Progress* and *The Rose and the Ring*—favorites of hers when she was my age. I would visit townspeople like the old women on Church and Main streets, women who knew stories about my great-grandfather Frank Russell. They would invite me in and fix me a bowl of ice cream topped with a sugar wafer, and while I ate they would tell me about all the folks he taught when he was a schoolteacher there and the dangerous roads he traveled when he sold goods, and they would go on to talk about their own dead husbands and the Daughters of the American Revolution.

My mother handed me a box wrapped with the Sunday funnies, so I knew it was from her. I smiled when I opened it. Inside the box was a pair of neatly folded lime green knee socks. The ribbed kind.

Already I had presented her with the pinecone wreath I'd spray-painted at school, but I also gave her a framed photo I'd taken of Willa Mae in front of our house. She seemed to like this and showed everyone.

I missed Perry then, and Willa Mae too, wishing they were both there, because when they were with us my mother and I were both always so much happier. I thought of Mary Alice then too, and of Stone and the McLemores and their Christmas morning in their tidy home. Their lives felt so far away from mine right now, and I suddenly saw the situation of my mother's life for what it was: My mother had left her own home in Virginia to marry, and then when her husband died, she felt she had to move to his family's home state. She was a stranger in a strange land.

My cousin Tine gave me another present marked with my name. I carefully opened the tiny square box. "Good things come in small packages," Aunt Ida said. I knew the gift was from my grandmother, but I was supposed to pretend it was from Santa Claus—for my younger cousins' sake or their parents', I didn't know which.

Inside the box was another box, a blue velvet box lined with satin the color of oyster shells, and there in the folds of the satin sat two perfect pearl earrings, the kind you could screw on.

"These belonged to my mother, your great-grandmother Irene," my grandmother said, moving next to me. "She and her family lost most everything in the war, but she managed to save a few things. Your mother and I think you're old enough now to have them." She didn't have to say it, but I knew my grandmother felt as though maybe I'd had the same kind of loss as Irene had.

Aunt Ida looked at the earrings over my shoulder and said, "Humph. My Tine has pierced ears, so she wouldn't want to wear those anyway."

My grandmother could cook. There was turkey and two kinds of cornbread stuffing—one with oysters, the other with pecans. There were sweet potatoes, lady peas, biscuits with fig preserves, fresh collard greens and fresh mustard greens from the garden. My mother put out choirboy and choirgirl angel candles. A wick came out of the tops of their head. They'd had these candles for as long as we could remember, none of us ever thinking to light the heads because, really, how could we?

No matter how old we were, cousins still sat at the kids' table, though we older ones served the grownups.

My grandfather said grace. Uncle Ted carved the turkey. Aunt Ida made toasts. Then everyone got to the eating.

"There's a new group in town called the Citizens' Council," Uncle Ted said, busy with his food. "Two dollars for membership. I know because they asked me to join. There's a businessman named McLemore in Jackson who's the ringleader."

I looked at my mother, waiting for her to say something. Everyone knew this new Citizens' Council group was up to no good.

"That's not true—I know that's not true," I said. "I know the McLemores. They're good people." I thought of Mary Alice, then said, "Most of them are."

"Listen, like I told you before over the phone, I happen to know your name is on their list," Uncle Ted told my mother, ignoring me. "And your house is being watched. You're hanging around the wrong sort. I hope your new *friend* isn't putting you in harm's way."

"Is he talking about Perry?" I asked.

"Hush, Sam," my mother said.

"Just stay with your own kind," Uncle Ted said to my mother. "I'm just trying to look out for you."

"How do you happen to know all this, Ted?" My grandmother stopped eating.

My grandfather looked at Ted. "You didn't join, son, did you?" He sounded surprised.

Uncle Ted cut into the turkey on his plate and smiled. "I'm not the enemy here."

"No?" my grandmother asked. "And exactly who is?"

"Look," he said, putting down his knife and fork. "This race problem, this isn't our battle."

"Whose is it then?" my grandmother asked.

"They're the country club KKK without the sheets," my grandfather went on. "You shouldn't have anything to do with them."

"They're nothing more than bad men in business suits." My grandmother touched her pearls. She looked to be calming herself down. "Herod is in Christmas," she said quietly. "Evil is there along with the good. My father used to remind me of that. 'Evil, resisting forces rising to destroy truth and love,' he'd say. That's the spirit of bigotry that is blind to everyone and everything. He knew a lot about evil, your grandfather Frank." She shook her head. "The Citizens' Council." She spat the words out. "That's not what this family is about."

Uncle Ted got up from the table and left the room. The

screen door slapped. The ceiling fans hummed. We all waited for his voice or more noise.

"Would you just look at those pretty birds outside," Aunt Ida said, taking a sip of sweet tea. "Pretty, pretty," she said, tapping her glass with her watermelon-colored nails.

My mother stood up to clear the table and motioned for me to do the same. She and I were usually the ones stuck doing the dishes. I chalked this up to the way my aunts and uncles felt about us. No one ever said so, but it seemed as though they thought my mother had been a mistake in my father's life. She was not from here, not even from the state. And now they were stuck with both her and me.

"Sit down, dears," my grandmother told us both, smoothing out the wrinkles in her dress with her hands. "We're not quite finished here. Children? When you're ready, there's coconut cake and pecan pie in the kitchen."

My cousins all went running into the kitchen. I stayed seated.

Aunt Ida changed the subject, asking about some woman from Franklin. "She's still smug over winning Miss Magnolia twenty years ago," she said. "I bet she's home right now, polishing that silver bowl."

"It was a tray," my grandmother said. "She won a tray."

"I always thought she got a crown," my mother said, smiling at my grandmother. I knew then that they liked each other, despite circumstances, despite what others might have thought. My mother often said she *respected* my grandmother, saying that she was "broad-minded," as though brains were to be measured like shoulders. But looking at them then, I thought, they just liked each other.

"Bowl, tray, crown, whatever she got. I pity her. I really do. She's troubled is what she is. Troubled." Aunt Ida chewed and chewed and chewed.

"You remind me so much of a woman I knew named Addy, Samantha. You two are cut from the same cloth." It was after the big feast, and the grownups were either napping or talking outside on the porch while my cousins went exploring in the woods. My grandmother and I were in the back guest room. She was going through her coat closet because she wanted to give my mother one of her coats. She thought my mother needed a coat. My grandmother had three closets for her clothes, one solely for her coats. Tine and I liked to scare ourselves opening this closet, because in it hung the red-brown fox, with its head still on and a tail that my grandmother let trail down her back. My grandmother said coats were the real reflection of a woman's wardrobe, and a woman could never have too many coats. My mother didn't even have a coat. She said people who lived in Mississippi didn't need coats.

Aunt Ida and Uncle Ted were in the adjoining bedroom, fighting. I was used to them arguing over his drinking or money or both. But on this day someone had switched on the radio. Martha and the Vandellas were singing, so I couldn't hear what they were arguing about.

"What happened to her?" I asked my grandmother. "What happened to Addy?"

"She could talk to the Choctaw and she learned from them. She became a nurse and a midwife," she said. "She helped birth a good portion of this county. I was her first delivery." She sighed and laughed. "Then later, when Addy grew older, she fell in love and married a man who was full-blooded Choctaw. They moved north to Neshoba County, where they set up a medical practice together. They had a son. She died of old age about three years ago."

I looked at my grandmother. Once upon a time she had been my age—a little girl running around getting dirty and into trouble. I had to wonder how anybody so old, polite, and mannerly managed to get along and survive in as hard a world as this. When exactly did the *growing up* part of growing up kick in?

"What are you two up to?" My mother came in with a cup of coffee.

"Shopping," my grandmother said. "Samantha and I think it's high time you went shopping for some new clothes."

"Honestly, I'm too busy to think about clothes."

"She's got Greece and Aphrodite on the brain," I joked, lying back on the bed and staring up at the white glossy paint peeling off the ceiling.

My grandmother laughed. "Aphrodite. For goodness' sake. What am I supposed to tell my friends in Culture Club?" My grandmother was joking and being serious at the same time. She could do that, though I was never sure how.

My cousin Tine and I used to eat the leftover butter mints from the little bowls my grandmother set out for Culture Club meetings. These ladies would get together and discuss books, plays, and paintings, or make perfectly cut flower arrangements, carefully clipping away the tendrils and stray vines.

"Now, here's a good running-around coat," she said, giving my mother a dark blue coat. "You could be Zeus in that coat." I put my head in my mother's lap. She traced the edges of my ear while I listened, and she and my grandmother went on talking.

That evening the middling cousins played Parcheesi, the older boys crept to the back of the house to look through back issues of *National Geographic,* and the rest of us cousins kicked off our shoes and socks and watched TV. In the shows everything happened very fast. The mistakes, the arguments, and then finally the hugging and the quick need to say "I love you."

During commercial breaks, Aunt Ida whispered her gossip, and the conclusions were all the same: *She doesn't know better,* which meant *She doesn't know her place,* which meant *She's gone beyond her raising.* Staying put as you were and with what you had was of primary importance. Even if we weren't listening, we cousins were meant to hear all of this.

CHAPTER 10

WE LEFT EARLY THE FOLLOWING MORNING, the morning after Christmas Day and my birthday, while everyone slept. She didn't tell me because she didn't have to, but I knew my mother never liked saying goodbye.

On the back seat of our VW Bug sat a box full of peach, pear, and plum preserves with masking tape labels made out in my grandmother's neat script. Next to the box of jars sat a bundle of my cousin Tine's old clothes folded neatly inside a shopping bag from Maison Blanche in New Orleans. In previous years, Aunt Ida had my mother sort through these clothes with me on the guest bed, and I was supposed to get all worked up over each item she pulled from the bag. My mother must have said something, because this year Aunt Ida secretly put the bag there in the back seat.

As we passed through Franklin, I read the sign on the store advertising bait: OUR WORMS CATCH FISH OR DIE TRYING. A new love song was playing on the car radio.

"Find something better," my mother said. "I hate that song."

I switched the station to a song played with a guitar, asking where all the flowers went. We drove in silence, staring out from our separate places. We passed through the colored section of town, where some lived in cinder-block homes with dirt floors and stuck colored bottles on the branches of trees stripped of foliage. My dad once told me that the bottles sucked in evil spirits called "haints." The rising sun shone through all that colored glass, and the wind whistled past the mouths of the bottles. I rolled down my car window to listen. Other people lived in nailed-together shacks with board floors. Some lived in shacks without windows or doors. Willa Mae told me once that the roofs often leaked in shacks like those, and the floors—if there were floors—often rotted. But we were used to these sights and this knowledge, or we were supposed to be used to it—the whites go here, the blacks there. Look out at a field and you half expected to see black people bent over picking cotton. It was the way things were.

Leaving Franklin, I thought of what it must have been like for my father to leave Franklin, and also what it must have been like for my mother to leave her hometown after she married.

"Why did you marry Dad, Mom?"

My mother sniffed through her nose, looked at me, then smiled.

"I wanted something more and he was it. We both had big dreams."

"Yeah?"

She nodded. "Yeah."

"So? Do you still?"

She shrugged. "Dreams get complicated."

"That must have taken a lot of courage," I said. "To marry Dad. He was so different from you."

"It was hardly courageous. It was just the only thing to do. We were in love."

We passed the smoking ruins of what could have been a church, and slowed only for a longer glimpse. We were getting used to seeing things smolder. Then we heard a police siren pop and my mother looked in her rearview mirror and pulled over.

"Oh, no," I said, holding on to the door handle, as though at any moment we could run for it.

"Was I speeding?"

I shook my head. "You were going slow."

"Maybe that's the problem."

The police officer walked slowly to our car, bent down, looked at my mother, and said, "Don't I know you? Who did you used to be?"

"Martha. Martha Thomas." She smiled. "I still am."

"That's right, that's right. I saw your picture in the paper. I knew your husband, Ed. We went to high school together. We played football. He was a good man, an outstanding quarterback."

He leaned in further and I saw his face. He was a handsome man about my mother's age, with blue eyes and a nice smile. "Don't believe I've met your daughter."

My mother told him my name and he tipped his hat my way.

They got talking. He joked about how he and my dad used to make away with watermelons from a nearby field, then crack them open on the road. He jiggled the keys and change in his pocket as he spoke. When he laughed, he put his tongue between his teeth and made a hissing sound. It smelled smoky outside. "He was a good man."

Finally, my mother asked why he'd stopped her.

"There's been a report of some trouble. Outsiders, most likely. Always is. Outsiders come in to stir up trouble."

So we weren't considered outsiders here. I wondered when exactly that had happened.

He knocked the hood of the car and told us to take care

and stay safe. "Let me know when you come back in town next," he said to my mother.

She smiled, and when I caught her looking at him from the rearview mirror, I joked that maybe moving back to Franklin wasn't such a bad idea after all.

"Not a chance," she said, speeding up. I don't know how I knew, but I knew then that she had her mind on Perry Walker.

CHAPTER 11

WHEN I OPENED THE MAIL I saw that I'd made okay grades, and as my mother read over my report card, she nodded and wondered out loud why there was no serious art instruction in the Jackson public school system and really no European history at all. My mother considered Europe the mother of all history, adding that you really couldn't study American anything until you had studied Europe.

"It looks like you all are spending a lot of time just talking about the South," she said.

I shrugged and asked if we had any potato chips. She

rolled her eyes, not because I asked, but because she knew that I knew we never ever had potato chips.

I watched my mother take in a deep breath and then let it out when she saw the C– for my communications grade. Miss Jenkins's comments about my state report also arrived with my grades. She pretty much said what she'd told me in front of the class: Nobody in my pictures was smiling. Nobody even looked happy. One might think that everybody who lived in Mississippi was sad, and was that really the way I wanted to represent our state in my report?

"She didn't get it, but that's not what you were going for," Perry said that night when he came over. He brought dinner this time, locking the door behind him, and he had pictures he'd just developed he wanted us to see. "You were going for art, not the grade."

"I wish I'd gotten an A." I felt like we were hunkering down in an air-raid shelter. It felt claustrophobic.

"You don't live in that world right now."

I didn't know what he was talking about. I was just getting angrier and angrier. I should have just done what all the others had done in my class—made dopey little collages and Elmer's-glued the cut-out pictures onto posterboard.

Perry showed us pictures he'd developed while we were gone, from a roll of film he had forgotten he had, long-distance shots unlike anything he was taking now. He showed us a picture he had taken of a subdivision much like ours from an airplane a friend of his flew—the subdivision looked like a giant octopus with its circle of streets like tentacles extending out.

"Sometimes you see the picture only later," he said, looking at the pictures spread out on the floor. It was as if he were looking at someone else's work, someone he didn't even know. "Way after you take the shot. Sometimes it's worth it to wait before you develop. Makes for a nice surprise."

"You're not still planning on going, are you?" my mother asked.

"Come with me," Perry said.

"I'll go," I said. They both looked at me. "You're talking about the day you're going to help black people register to vote, right? I want to go. I could help. Mom, you and me, we could both help. They need volunteers. Perry said so."

"It's not safe," my mother said.

Perry and I both just looked at my mother. We waited. She stood up and went into the kitchen, then called out and told me to go to bed.

We took Highway 55 and drove south to McComb. Perry and I both had our cameras hanging from our necks. On the way there, Perry told us about a black farmer named Herbert Lee who was shot in cold blood the year before because of his participation in voter registration. The murderer was E. H.

Hurst, a member of the Mississippi state legislature. Nobody ever charged Hurst with the crime.

"But that was in Liberty, not McComb," my mother said to me. I knew she was trying to reassure herself.

"Right," Perry said, but he thought we should also know about what had happened in McComb just the year before. More than one hundred high school students were jailed for protesting. One man was beat nearly to death by a mob of angry white men while police just stood by and FBI agents took notes.

"But that was last year," Perry said, finally turning on the radio. "All in the past." My mother didn't say much else for the rest of the ride down. McComb today wasn't going to be that different and we all knew it.

When we turned off the highway and in to McComb, volunteers and protesters were all already there in two straight, orderly lines, and they were kneeling on the concrete sidewalk as though in prayer. There were men and women, black and white, and even some kids my age. The women had their heads covered with scarves tied at their chins, and the men wore suits and ties. They'd hung posterboard signs around their necks saying THE TEST MUST GO! BALLOT FOR FREEDOM! WE WANT TO VOTE! A police car cruised along the street around them, circling them at about two miles an hour.

Winter was here, and a brown carpet of fallen pine needles united us all.

We followed Perry to someone with a stack of papers, who told us what to do. We were going door to door, handing out voter registration forms. All we had to do was say "Have you registered to vote?" and hand out a registration form. If the person needed help filling it out, we would help him or her read the form and fill it out.

I took a stack of papers and while my mother went to one house, I went to the one next door. We finished one block and then another, and soon we started on another. I was enjoying myself. A black woman, someone's maid, answered the knock. She looked at me while I talked about voting and registering, but then when I handed her the paper, she looked past me and mumbled "Oh Lord, have mercy" and shut the door. I turned around to see what she had seen.

Mobs of white men were closing in on the line of protesters, and as they did this they just started beating them with what they had—billy clubs, ax handles, and sticks—just as they had the year before. It all started so fast. Some punched and kicked, slinging people around, knocking them in the head. But none of the protesters fought back. Some of them ran into the streets, only to get chased by a white man with a stick. They just took it. They took the beating. It was nearly impossible to watch.

I saw Perry at the edge of the chaos, snapping picture after picture. I heard my mother calling my name, but I couldn't see her. I had my camera around my neck, so I lifted it and started taking pictures of police cars circling the beaters and the beaten. The police didn't even get out of their squad cars.

I lost sight of Perry then. I couldn't find my mother and I couldn't hear her calling for me anymore either. I was scared. I was angry. Willa Mae had told me to turn those feelings into something else. I lifted my camera and closed my left eye. It was as if the camera became a part of my eyes, a part of me, and my head and hands just followed, doing what they were told to do. Me? I disappeared, and so did my fear.

That's when I saw Stone, standing there in the green space that was a small park, away from the circle of craziness. I looked at what he was looking at—there was his father with a billy club, beating a man I had just seen kneeling with all the others.

Pickup trucks and paddy wagons came and the police finally got out of their cars, only to begin loading the bloodied protesters. Most were limping. Some looked to have broken ribs or legs. They were under arrest now for disturbing the peace.

As I crossed the street, Stone turned his head and saw me.

"Samantha, get back," he shouted, waving his hands for me to go away.

But then, all at once, I was part of the crowd of protesters. I couldn't see where I was going. I was shorter than everyone else. I could only smell the crush of all those bloody, sweating bodies. All around me stood men, black and white, knots swelling on their heads and blood running. White men were shoving these men into the paddy wagons and pickup trucks, pushing them as if they were cattle. Children were getting crammed in too, even women carrying crying babies. I thought then of what Ears had said one day outside at school. This was like something out of the Bible. But surely because this was so unjust, any minute someone would come and right this wrong. Any minute now.

If I'd had an enlarger like the one Perry had in his darkroom, I'd have taken this high-speed moment and printed it bigger, making the contrasts in black and white even more vivid. Now more than ever it was so clear to me what was right and what was wrong.

At the doors of one paddy wagon I saw Mr. McLemore shoving people in. I called his name. He looked at me but then looked right through me. I could see that I too would be shoved in, and I simply prepared myself for just that. I understood what that expression *brace yourself* meant then. I was ready for anything, because I saw then that the *someones* to come and right this wrong were in fact us, this line of people getting shoved into paddy wagons.

If all those white men were this scared and angry over black people registering to vote, then voting must be a powerful, powerful weapon.

"Samantha!" Stone was there, right by me.

"Step aside, son," Mr. McLemore said, tapping Stone's chest with his club. "That girl's one of them."

Stone shook his head. "No. No she's not."

"Son," Mr. McLemore said. He tapped his club on Stone's arm. "Don't you dare cross me."

Stone just took my hand and snatched me out, leading me away. I kept looking back, expecting someone to come after us, but nobody did. I was both relieved and angry that Stone had pulled me away. I was still wearing the cross necklace he had given me, but I didn't want to think of Stone in that way right then.

Perry and my mother came running toward Stone and me.

"Thank God you're all right," my mother said, hugging me, moving me away from Stone. We heard sirens then. Somebody had set a house on fire across the street. What else could happen? Perry reloaded his camera and made to go toward the house, but my mother held his arm.

"No. We're going. Now," she said.

Perry nodded, said "Right," then put his arm around me and around Stone too.

"No," my mother said. "Not with him. Not with that boy."

"But Mom. Stone got me out . . ."

"That's okay, Mr. Walker. I've got a ride back."

Perry looked at Stone and let his arm drop. We three just started walking back to the car, none of us saying anything. What was there left to say?

As I fell asleep that night and many other nights that week after Christmas, I prayed I wouldn't have to write an essay called "What I Did over the Holidays." I kept hearing Miss Jenkins's fake-peppy voice singing, *"Go, Mississippi, you're on the right track. Go, Mississippi, and this is a fact, Go, Mississippi, you'll never look back."* Never look back? Didn't everyone in this state talk about The War every other day? And then there was that last part of the song when you spell it, and we all knew that we would spend the rest of our lives singing the spelling: *"M-I-S-S-I-S-S-I-P-P-I!"*

CHAPTER 12

AT SCHOOL, MARY ALICE TOLD EVERYBODY that her father had given her little brother, Jeffy, a BB gun for Christmas and her mother bought her a brand-new portable TV so she could watch programs all day from her bed. It was an altogether new television season and a new year. 1963.

Talk of the New Year only made my mother irritated with everything and everybody, especially me. Why couldn't I pick up my room? she wanted to know. I was spoiled because I didn't like any of Tine's old hand-me-downs, clothes that to me looked like costumes my Aunt Ida put together.

I knew the real reason my mother was testy. Perry hadn't

called since he'd dropped us off at home after our trip to McComb, and I think she was realizing what I already knew: She liked him. She liked him a lot.

But she was also angry with him. It really had been dangerous in McComb. Out-of-state newspapers and TV news crews were coming into town now and reporting on what had happened there. What had happened in McComb was happening in other small towns all over the state—both the voters registering and the rioting. On the news, we watched little white boys turning a hose on an old black woman while grown white people just stood by and watched.

When the phone finally did ring, though, it wasn't Perry. It was Stone. He wanted to know if he could take me to the Petrified Forest. I hadn't been there since my grandparents took me one summer when I was little. Stone *had* rescued me, in a way, that day in McComb less than a week ago. Surely there must be a good explanation for him being there that day. I needed to talk to him in person. I pleaded with my mother to let me go with him. Finally she agreed.

Before he came to pick me up late that Saturday afternoon, I dressed carefully. I wore my own sweater and skirt. I wore the gold cross necklace Stone had given me. I clipped on the earrings my grandmother had given me for Christmas.

The Petrified Forest wasn't very far from where we lived, and when we got there, we sat on the bench from prehistoric times called the Caveman's Bench.

"This must have been something when these stone logs were living trees. They must have been huge," I said, but Stone was looking up at the sky. Already the stars were out. Even though our teachers called these woods Mississippi's own Grand Canyon, most kids my age tended to take the Petrified Forest for granted. They walked these woods every spring on field trips.

"I love to come out here and look at the sky," Stone said. "This could be the best, most quietest place I know. See? See all the stars you can already see?"

I turned to him then. "I need to know something for sure, Stone. Are you a member of that Citizens' Council with your dad?"

He looked up at the sky. "I'm not my father."

"I know that. But are you a member?"

The air was crisp and smelled of burning leaves. Somewhere up in the trees, an owl called.

"That was a bad day in McComb, and my father . . ." Stone stopped himself. "My father wasn't himself." Stone switched the subject. He talked about the dark side of the moon and other unmapped territories.

"Why was your dad so mad? Why does he hate black people so much?"

"He gets that way. I don't know. He doesn't like what's happening. He doesn't like change. And he really doesn't like outsiders coming in and changing things."

"Outsiders like my mom and me?"

"Y'all are different."

"Like Perry, then. He's an outsider."

"Yes, he is."

"So what if he is?"

"My dad thinks he stirs up trouble."

"Do you?"

"I don't know what to think anymore."

If the cicadas lived longer, they would have been humming loud all around us, making a racket, because I thought I heard them, in my head. I thought about prehistoric crawdads and turtles crawling up from the stream. Then I thought of what all had happened or could happen here, acts of violence that never made the news. Only last year a black man had been lynched in these very woods. On the nearby highway, a black mother of three had been raped, and then shot in the head. And there we were.

Stone pointed out the Big Dipper and the Little Dipper. He talked about altitudes and zeniths.

"Stone. Everything's crazy right now. Can't you think of anything else but constellations?"

"Things'll settle down."

"Or maybe they'll get worse before they get better."

Stone shook his head. "No way they can get worse. Everybody will learn they don't want to live like this and then we'll go back to the way things were."

I thought about that. "What if nobody wants that? What if nobody wants things the way things were? Black people you and me both know can't vote, and they'll keep on making next to nothing, raising their families in little shacks. That's the way things are. You think that's right?"

He sighed and fell back onto the ground, which was covered with soft dry pine needles. "I don't know, Samantha. I don't know." He pulled me down with him and hugged me tight, something he had never done before. Stone had a sour smell. I did not know where it was coming from, just that his odor had changed.

I could feel his chest against me. He put his face close to mine. He kissed my lips. Then we both kissed, this time together. It was a slow, sweet kiss, not one of those messy, lippy wet kisses with tongues I'd seen in the backs of buses and movie houses. And I didn't know that my eyes would close automatically, but they did this time, and when I opened them only because I didn't want to miss seeing this, his eyes were open too, and we just stayed together like that, our lips kissed swollen.

Thumb-size beetles scurried around us among the leaves.

"Damn them." Stone got up off the ground. He kicked each leg to shake his pants down. Then he started stepping on the beetles, smashing them with his boots. I thought of my mother's word *primordial* then. Beetles were like cicadas—

both looked to be little armored dinosaurs. Up close, you could see all their jewel-like colors too.

"They're not bothering anything," I said.

"They're pests."

"No, they're not," I said. "Besides, they'll just keep coming."

"Not if we stop them."

He walked around stomping and stomping, all the while looking at me and smiling. I tried not to mind all that crunching, but my heart stopped.

Then Stone finally stopped and smoothed his hair up and back with a comb the way everyone's seen James Dean do. I touched my earlobes.

"My earrings!" I started feeling around in the pine needles. "They're gone. They belonged to my great-grandmother."

Stone and I knelt for some time, feeling among the leaves and pine needles and dead beetles, but it was so dark, it was hopeless.

"Don't worry, sweetie," he said. "I'll get you a new pair."

A new pair? The idea of replacing my only inherited heirloom knocked the words right out of me. I couldn't think of what to say, so I said nothing. My ears felt raw, like the feeling your toes have right after you cut your toenails.

I stayed on the ground, crawling and feeling around. Under a bush, my fingers curled around something that felt a lot like a camera.

"This is Perry's," I said, surprised. It was the small camera Perry had shown me in his darkroom at the university, the one he said he'd used to photograph the military hospital in D.C. I looked closely and saw that the lens was cracked and the body of the camera was dented too, but it was still loaded with film.

"Why would Perry's camera be here?" Stone said, helping me up. "And how come it's smashed?"

"I know he comes here a lot to take pictures," I said. "Maybe it fell out of his camera bag."

Stone started to reach for the camera to have a look, but I put it in the pocket of my jacket, hardly thinking about it. Stone just stood there, looking at me and then at my jacket pocket, back and forth. I smiled. "I'll just give it to him next time he comes over," I said.

Stone took me back home. He didn't say anything more about the earrings. I didn't know how I would face my mother or my grandmother, knowing I'd lost the pearl earrings. Stone didn't seem too upset. His mind was on something else. He turned on the car radio. Elvis was playing, "Don't Be Cruel." Stone drove on, and I sat there in the passenger seat knowing I'd left behind something my ancestors had saved just for me—I'd lost them, just like that, kissing a boy.

I tried to forget about the earrings. I kept singing the words to that Elvis song in my head as though convincing myself of something: *"The future looks bright ahead."*

CHAPTER 13

MY MOTHER GOT THE CALL THE FOLLOWING MORNING. She hung up the phone, and then she went to the back door and looked out the screen. Her shoulders were shaking and I knew she was crying.

We both went to the hospital.

A machine behind his bed beeped and plastic tubes hung from a stainless-steel bar, one half filled with blood. An IV tube dripped some clear liquid into his arm, and the gauze wrapped around his forehead was stained with his browning blood. I wanted so badly for him to wake up and joke, look at my mother that way that made her happy, but Perry just lay there swollen shut, unable to move or speak.

Somebody had beat him and beat him and beat him. Somebody had kicked his ribs, his legs, and his head. I heard the nurse whisper to my mother that Perry had head trauma, brain swelling, facial lacerations, and cracked ribs. Both his legs were in casts, his kneecaps shattered. Both his eyes were swollen shut as though whoever attacked him never wanted him to see again. Whoever did this had left him on the sidewalk in front of the newspaper building, a warning to journalists, even though the local paper never even printed any of Perry's photographs.

There was a lot of internal bleeding. My mother choked on those words.

She sat back down in the chair next to his bed. She held on to the fingers poking out of the bandages on his left hand. She squeezed them.

I tried not thinking about Stone kissing me until my lips swelled just the night before. I tried not imagining his hands on me, or what he looked like, smiling, standing up, there in the woods. I told myself not to care, because now was not the time for such thoughts.

Perry was my mother's friend. He was her boyfriend. She loved him, even though it was so hard to love anybody else after loving my dad. I think I knew this before she did. He was also my friend. He had given me his camera. Even though my mother went through all the reasons Perry shouldn't have given me his old camera, he still did. He told us his camera was like him. Indestructible.

We stayed all day. We closed our eyes and prayed, which we had not done together in a long time. The nurse came in and out of the room. Everything felt awful and I wondered why the whole world didn't seem to notice how bad things really were. I thought of how I'd gotten used to awful, how after my dad died the planets kept on spinning and I got up and ate breakfast every morning and kept on going to school. Something happens and it's terrible and you think you can't live another day, but then your mother gets used to it and you get used to it and you both keep on living, and you're not sure if that getting-used-to-things is good or the way life should be.

We visited Perry at the hospital every day that week. One day the nurses said he was a little better. The next day they said he was worse.

Driving to and from the hospital, my mother and I couldn't help but notice that Jackson looked like a war zone. Most everyone, black and white, was complaining about what a mess Mississippi had become. It was as if they were spending so much time scheming over the "black problem" that they weren't thinking about how to fix potholes, schools, abandoned houses, and burned-out buildings. For days we came home tired, eating tomato soup and crackers or bowls of cereal for dinner.

We both heard and read about ongoing investigations into Perry's attack. There were leads and suspects. Then on Friday, we read in the paper that they had arrested a man, a black man.

"They're saying this man didn't want Perry taking his picture trying to register to vote because it would hurt his family," my mother said, sitting there next to Perry, reading from the paper, shaking her head. "They're saying he went to Perry's place, broke in, took him away, and beat him."

I shook my head. "That's crazy," I whispered. I had started to whisper everything. "I don't believe any of that." I felt now I knew what the word *unspeakable* really meant.

Perry stopped breathing on a beautiful sunny Sunday afternoon when the whole world seemed to be coming out of a deep sleep. My mother swore he squeezed her hand, and I believed her.

We were both there. Already it was warm outside, but the light was fading as the sun went down into the wet streets, and we could smell the warm rolls and the green beans getting served for dinner up and down the hospital corridor. It was as though the sun itself were taking Perry away, and when he was gone the room went dark and the hospital's air conditioner sighed. I had been wrong not to trust Perry with my mother at the beginning, just because he was an outsider and different from any other man I had known. We all were different, and that made us all the same.

"He didn't have anybody but us," my mother said as we looked out the window and watched the sun going down from Perry's hospital room. "No family." Her eyes were red from crying. I couldn't help it. I started crying too.

"We need to go to his place," my mother said. "Make sure everything's turned off, see if there's anyone to contact." I could tell she was trying to get organized and make sense of what had happened. She'd done this when my dad died too. I could tell she was thinking, *Maybe I can still fix this.*

"This is my fault," I said, crying harder. "I told. I did it. I told Stone about the people going to register." I was crying so hard then, snot ran out of my nose. I was crying so hard, I scared myself. But it was my mess. I'd made the mess. *Loose lips sink ships.* They do. They do. It was my fault. All of this was my fault.

"This is not your fault, do you understand me?" my mother said. She was fierce, holding my head, looking me in the eye.

When she said it like that I felt better and worse all at once. Better because she was so sure and she was forgiving me, worse because her forgiveness made me feel worse and even uglier with guilt.

"I lost my earrings too, Mom. I'm no good. I'm no good at all."

"Oh, honey. Don't worry about the earrings, okay? This wasn't your fault."

Everywhere around me sounds became stainless-steel sharp, their edges scraping against my eyes and ears. All I wanted to do was sleep in a dark, noiseless room. I didn't want to hear any more voices. I needed a place to hide, but there was no such place. Everywhere I turned that night and in the days to come, a voice was too loud, a car door slamming too noisily.

What would my dad have said? Would he have wanted us to stay and fight this out, fight other people's battles? Or go, just go? Leave and be safe? Wouldn't he want us to be safe?

"They don't have the right murderer," I whispered.

"I know," my mother said. "I know."

I already had one death in my life. My dad's. And now there was Perry. And that afternoon, the afternoon Perry died, I knew that my mother and I cried for them both. We slept together that night, holding each other, wordless. We stayed still like that with our eyes shut. In my dreams, I saw us together like that, with something like chords of sound linking us, running back and forth between our heads, carrying words only we could understand.

CHAPTER 14

MY MOTHER HAD JUST DRIVEN WILLA MAE HOME when my grandmother arrived. She drove all the way in just to be with us. I
heard my mother tell her she was worried about me.

My grandmother tied on an apron, took out our black skillet, and first cooked some bacon, then scrambled some eggs
in the leftover grease. She put one of Willa Mae's good biscuits on my plate, and I moved it so that it could soak up
some of the bacon grease on the bottom the way I liked.
Then we sat down at the table together and ate. She told me
she would stay the week to look after us.

In my room, she rocked me in her arms as we sat on my bed.

"You're grieving, sweetie. And you're scared. That's all it is," she said. "We're living in scary times." I watched her looking at all of Perry's photographs I'd taped to my walls.

There was so much you could see in those pictures—the baker in the baker's shop smiling at the woman in another shop and the way they looked at each other, you knew, you just knew how much they liked each other. Who knew if it would last, but for that second it was everything.

He had taken pictures of coal miners, of young men hauling bricks on their shoulders, of boys mining, and of a boy going off to school with his knapsack in Germany, his town and streets in ruins. I thought it looked a little like Jackson.

There was the picture of my mother and me side by side the night I dressed up to look like her for Mary Alice's party, my mother's arm reaching out over me.

Perry's pictures showed so much of how people were together, how mothers were when they raised their children, how much they held us and cuddled us, how close we could be when we let closeness happen.

At school Mary Alice wore new saddle shoes, but for the first time I didn't care what Mary Alice wore.

After Perry's funeral, my mother spent most of her time up at the college.

The faculty at my mother's college voted to support the

ministers in town who were concerned about being able to speak freely in churches and schools. The faculty resolved that there should be nothing now to deny people in Mississippi of their right to freedom of speech, because it was a fact that we still lived in a democracy.

My mother said that there was a lot of tension in her school and around town, and we both needed to be more careful than ever.

School kept on being school. Mary Alice was making friends with a new girl in the tenth grade who looked a lot like a new doll I'd seen advertised. They both wore the same kind of saddle shoes.

I stayed in my room and stared at the shadows made from my bedside lamp, the slats on the blinds, the sliver of light from an open door. Mourning Perry felt a lot like sleepwalking or like your eyes getting used to the dark. I didn't say much. I couldn't listen to music. I could imagine myself humming again, but I couldn't imagine forming words. I thought about forgetting altogether how to talk. *Voice* was so close to the word *void*.

Where we lived in Mississippi, February was spring. In the morning sheets of ground fog cloaked the lawns and trees. Mary Alice took to parting her hair on the side and rolling her skirts up at the waist to make them shorter. In the hall, she bumped into me and accidentally-on-purpose spilled the contents of her purse, showing everybody that she carried around a bottle of perfume and a spare Kotex—just to let everyone know that she was woman enough to smell nice and have menstrual cramps too. This time, some of us girls didn't want to keep up with Mary Alice anymore.

At school we learned some about the Choctaw, the Algonquians, the Chickasaw, the Natchez, and the Pascagoula Indians.

"They never wrote their history," Miss Jenkins said. "So to most, it doesn't count."

That couldn't be true, I thought. And it was crazy if it was true. Their history helped make history. Once you did something important, was it as important to make noise about it? This time I knew better than to say what I thought.

"Keeping a record is important," Miss Jenkins said.

I thought about Perry's pictures of my mother, the ones of her walking back and forth in the living room while he stood outside taking the pictures. In them she looked like a ghost. Was everything a record? And if so, what were those pictures a record of?

I thought about that night at my mother's party when I heard Perry talking to her about why he had to go to McComb to help register voters. He said it was because he was a human being. And I thought about what that man said to Perry in the corner of the room. He said: "We need somebody with a camera." What he was saying was: *We need a witness. We need someone to go out and show the world what's going on down here so it can stop, get fixed, get sorted out. We need eyeballs, brains, mouths, hands—we need to get the word out anyhow and anyway. We need pictures and stories.* Miss Jenkins was right. Keeping a record was important. Just as there were some in Mississippi who really wanted the rest of the world to stay out or forget we were here, there were others in the state shouting out, *Hey! Here we are, and terrible things are happening! Pay attention!*

That afternoon after school, when I put on my coat, I felt the camera there in the pocket. Perry's camera, the one I found that day I went with Stone to the Petrified Forest. I rushed to my mother's school and ran up the steps to her office. She was with a student, and I paced the halls, waiting for her. When the student left, I tapped on her door.

"Mom," I said. "I need to use Perry's darkroom."

"Now?"

I put my hands in my coat pocket and felt for the camera again. I had a feeling.

I nodded. My mother didn't even ask. It was as if she knew. It was as if we didn't need words anymore. She looked around. She stood up and looked up and down the hall. "All right, but not the one here. That's for students only, and I don't need to get into any more trouble." She put on her coat, the one my grandmother had given her. "I'm finished grading. Let's go to Perry's. I still haven't sorted through his things."

CHAPTER 15

PERRY HAD LIVED IN THE POOR PART OF TOWN, where he'd started an afterschool photography program for young people. He never locked his door. He would have said *Come in* to anyone who knocked. My mother had already gone there alone to find what she could of people to contact. There really had been nobody else in his family, nobody else but us, because now more than ever we felt like Perry's family. We passed the twigs that were his hydrangea bushes. I tried to picture how they would be in the summer, their face-size blue blooms drooping again with morning dew.

His jacket hung on a hook. His bed was unmade. There

was a camera on the kitchen table with extra rolls of film and spare lenses. *Life* magazines laid open on the coffee table near a full ashtray, an open bottle of cream soda, and an advance copy of the photography book he was working on with a publisher in New York. The pillows on the sofa were smooshed and dented with the shape of his back and head. It felt as though he had just gone out for milk or bread and that he would be back any minute.

Except that he wouldn't.

We didn't say anything. It didn't feel right to talk.

The world felt so sad at that moment as we looked around Perry Walker's room. And outside, Jackson felt only small and tight and airless.

"Completely senseless," I heard my mother say as she began to clean up.

I fingered the camera still in my jacket pocket, then pulled it out. Here was one of Perry's cameras, and it was still loaded with film. While my mother began putting dishes in a box for Goodwill, I slipped into Perry's darkroom.

The pans were neatly lined up in the tiny darkroom and all along the walls on built-in shelves were instruments to enable a person to look more closely at the world: lighting devices for his cameras, rolls of what looked like Saran wrap, tarps, extra film, light bulbs, and more cameras.

All around me, Perry's unframed black-and-white pictures hung on the walls—pictures of people behind bars in prison, people in wheelchairs, homeless people asleep in strange city streets, dirty, naked children begging for food in front of grocery stores with foreign names, dying or dead soldiers left in the mud. A picture can do so much, he'd once told me. If it's a picture of someone singing, you can hear the music.

Hanging on one line were the last pictures Perry had developed—the pictures from that day in McComb with all the protesters on their knees, and then being pushed and shoved into the paddy wagons.

I don't know what I thought I would find in there or in the pictures I was about to develop, but I knew that I had to see and find out. Perry once told me that it was important to have motivation or purpose behind your work. That's what this feeling I had felt like: it felt purposeful.

I did and did not know what I was doing. When I saw how fuzzy these new images first were, I thought I'd made a mistake, but then I saw they were blurry for a reason. Perry had just snapped and snapped, not bothering or unable to hold the camera still. Just get the shot. That was always his number one recommendation.

The pictures showed the story. Fists and hands carrying clubs, sticks, and rocks coming toward me, the viewer, the camera lens. It must have been hard to keep taking the pictures. He must have kept the camera off to the side. It was still light out, so he hadn't needed a flash. There must have been so much shouting and noise, they hadn't heard the clicking. He'd made a decision. He decided to use his one hand not to fight but to take pictures.

Oh, but they hated him, and they wanted him suffering and dead from their own beating. They called themselves Christian and hid behind their own white churches. Hadn't they read the Bible? Didn't they know about Jesus? If they saw these pictures clearly in black and white for themselves, surely they'd see what they had done. It was a scene straight out of the Bible, like an art slide from one of my mother's lectures, the one she gave at Tougaloo about martyrs.

Then I looked closer at one of the pictures still developing. At first, all I could see were arms—all of them strong and white and male, but then I saw a face I recognized emerging in the pan of water. I saw the profile, the nose, the strong chin, and the hate in his eyes. I recognized that look. It was the same look his son Stone had when he was stomping out bugs. And there he was with that angry face, waving a billy club: there was Mr. McLemore.

Had he really done this? And what was Stone's involvement? Had he stood by and watched, then done nothing? Or had he tried to stand up to these men as he had stood up to his father and saved me in McComb?

But then, why would Stone have allowed me to take and keep Perry's camera? Maybe he wanted me to know. Maybe he wanted me to see for myself what he couldn't admit about his father and maybe about himself. Maybe letting me keep the camera was Stone's way of confessing.

It came slow, but it all became clear to me, as gradual as the appearance of that picture on the blank sheet of paper.

I found Perry's camera at the Petrified Forest, where they must have taken him. They had done this. Stone and his father and their terrible group had done this. They had taken a man to a place to be beaten, then Stone had taken me there to that same place to be kissed.

Was it really possible that this boy I'd kissed was also someone who beat and kicked a human being to death? It took a gazillion years for those trees in that forest to transform into something they were not, but what I wanted to know now was how long exactly did it take for a human heart to turn to stone?

And how could people you know, people you thought to be good, people who were busy, working people, neighbors, how could they do these kinds of things? How can murder happen in the everyday? How can a man be beaten to death while nearby others talked, ate sandwiches, did the dishes, put clothes out to dry, or kissed? How?

Did good happen the same way? Could an angel fall from the sky while Willa Mae made tuna salad? Could help come on horseback or in a squad car while I was skipping rope?

You're traveling through another dimension. . . . That's the signpost up ahead—your next stop . . . I might as well have been in a *Twilight Zone* episode—maybe the one in which they are all on a plane that accidentally breaks the sound barrier and they can't land because the year is not their year, but in my show, I'd land and the year I'd land in would be the future. Because I needed to know. I needed to know that things were changed, different, and better, not like this. Not worse.

All I wanted to do was fight this hate with my own rising hate. I wanted to hunt Stone down myself, slap him, and kick him even. Because really, didn't it take murder and violence to knock some people to their senses?

Outside the wind was blowing, and the hard leaves of the magnolia snapped against one another. Here was this beautiful world, so why were people messing with it?

I stared at all the pictures hanging on the line. Here was proof that the police had arrested the wrong man. What now? Who could I trust with them? I couldn't give them to the police or to the newspaper.

I left Perry's darkroom to find my mother on the sofa, weeping, Perry's photographs of her and us in her lap. I went to her and we held each other.

"This will all be over soon," she said. "It just can't keep on and on, that's all. You'll see. Soon, we'll hardly remember any of this." I know she meant for that to sound like a good thing, not remembering what had happened and was still happening, but I didn't want to forget.

It seemed to me that what James Meredith and Perry Walker and all the others did, what they had witnessed and lived through, what they sometimes died for, was of greater benefit to us than all the satellites and *Sputniks* being put into space. Their courage went beyond the courage of the cosmonauts or astronauts. I doubted I would ever have that kind of courage.

I thought of them all. I thought of my dad and even people I'd never met—my great-grandfather Frank Russell and all the Choctaw who had been moved, plowed, or lived over. I used to think the dead went away as if they were going on vacation to Florida or somewhere else nice. Then I began thinking they might stay closer to home. They were with us and they were not with us. They reminded us. They kept us company. They could be our friends or our foes—we decided. I wondered if Perry would haunt the McLemores. He wouldn't be scared to. After all, ghosts couldn't die.

CHAPTER 16

AFTER I SHOWED MY MOTHER THE PICTURES I'd developed in Perry's darkroom, she wondered out loud what we should do. We hurried home and we showed my grandmother.

I had two folders full. I watched my grandmother's face as she looked through them. It was odd; I felt as if she shouldn't see them, as though they would be too much for her. I wanted to protect her from their badness.

Anybody could look through these and make out the struggle—the arms, the fists, the billy clubs. In the pictures, the men doing the hitting were smiling. Some of the faces were blurry, but some were clear and in focus. I looked for

Stone, but I couldn't see him. Had he been there? If he had, he could have stopped them. If Stone was so strong, he could have tried and stopped them all.

I wanted to ask my grandmother, *How could this happen?* But it felt good just to be close to her, to feel her long arms around me.

"Their good time is coming to an end," she said, after a while. "They see it, and that's what the matter is." She sounded so old and tired. I felt terrible for showing her the pictures.

How can we fix this? How can we fix this? I thought over and over.

I got up and went to the phone.

"Who are you calling?" my mother asked.

"Stone."

"Is that wise?"

I sighed. "Probably not, but he needs to know."

When he came to our front door that night, he looked surprised to see my mother and grandmother with me. I didn't beat around the bush. I just gave him the folders full of pictures, saying, "Remember that camera we both found at the Petrified Forest?"

Stone saw what we'd already seen.

"What are you going to do?" he said, looking at the three of us.

"What do you want us to do, Stone?" my mother asked.

He closed his eyes for a minute and took a deep breath. "We should take these to the police."

"I'll take them myself," I started.

"No," he said. "I should. I should take these to the police. I don't want you to get into any more danger. There are some people who shouldn't know you have these."

"So," I said. My voice came out flat. "You *were* there."

"No. I wasn't."

"Stone, you don't have to—"

"With all due respect, Mrs. Thomas, I really do have to. They wouldn't believe you, but I'm his son."

"Well, son, with all due respect to you . . ." my grandmother said, taking the pictures from Stone, putting all that hate back in the folders. I thought at first she would tuck them away somewhere, under a bed or in a closet, where all boogeymen and scary things go to be hidden and forgotten. She smoothed her dress over her knees and held the folders on her lap. "How about we have Samantha develop two sets of prints. You have your copies, we have our copies. It's not that we don't trust you to do the right thing, mind you. It's just"—she hesitated—"insurance." She stood up. She looked tall all of a sudden. "A man's dead and the wrong man is in jail." She went to the phone and dialed. No one asked whom she was calling. "Sit on the truth too long and you mash the life right out of it."

"I understand, ma'am, but there's no time to make copies."

"Sam's got the negatives," my mother said.

"We'll go with you to the station anyway. I'll drive. We go where the pictures go."

"Grandmother."

"Your grandmother's right, Samantha." Stone stood up. "Let's go."

We all piled into my grandmother's big clean car, a car she called her Dinah Shore Chevy, which she had bought sometime in the fifties. She insisted on driving, offering us each Butter Rum Lifesavers from her purse as though they would give us strength and keep us safe for the ride ahead.

We headed downtown, toward the police station.

Inside the station, police officers looked through all the pictures, their faces turning to frowns. This time there was solid evidence and witnesses to that evidence. They said they would have to keep a few of the photos and Stone for further questioning.

"Can they do that?" I asked my mother.

"I'm afraid they can."

"Leave me," Stone said to my mother, my grandmother, and me. He looked at me then and smiled.

"I'll call your mother," my mother said.

"No," he said. "Really. That isn't important."

I hated that we had to leave Stone there in that place, but when we looked back at him, I was surprised to see him look relieved. His jaw unclenched, and he didn't look angry anymore.

Inside the car, my grandmother said we had one more stop to make, a thirty-minute drive from where we were then.

"Where?" I asked.

"Mother, are you sure about this?" my mother asked. She was up front in the passenger's seat.

"What are we doing?" I said.

"No need to know until we get there," my grandmother said. "That way, if someone stops us, you won't have to lie."

"What in the world is going on?"

"Samantha," my mother said, turning around from the front seat. "You're just going to have to trust us just like you trusted Stone."

My grandmother never really caught on to driving, maybe because she was unsure about women driving at all. Whenever she set out to drive, my grandfather would call after her, "Watch out for all that vehicular traffic!" But that never did her much good. She would slow down at green lights and whiz past red ones. She had not gotten into an accident yet because when they saw her coming down the road, everyone in Franklin pulled by the side of the road as though she were an ambulance. But we were outside of Franklin now.

She hated going over bridges because she was scared of heights, so when we drove over the Pearl River she had to sing "Amazing Grace," which only put my mother to sleep.

After we crossed the last bridge, my grandmother looked at me in the rearview mirror. My mother was still asleep. She signaled and turned on to another highway. "You know what my father used to tell me, back when I was growing up?" She sighed, and then she laughed outright. "He said, 'Thelma Addy. Being right is right lonely.'"

She laughed again. "My father was right. But being wrong and doing nothing is worst of all."

My grandmother drove on, turning off the highway, then stopping in front of a little white house with green shutters and a big front porch. There were so many woods and back roads and little unnamed pockets in these parts, it was easy to have and keep secrets here. A man with a dog sat in a rocking chair. He stood up when he saw my grandmother's car. My mother woke up, groggy. He asked us all up to the porch and they talked, this man and my grandmother. They were friends from way back. My mother and I sat and listened. They could have been kin for all that they had in common. My grandmother gave him the folders. He looked at the pictures.

"Sometimes I think to understand Mississippi, you have to live here a hundred years," he said, looking through them once, twice, then stacking them neatly again. The oscillating porch fan whirred as we waited. "Samantha, I run a small newspaper that's getting some attention up north, maybe because we report the truth. Truth is hard to find down here. Us southerners tend to bury everything, then kudzu grows up over it. Perry Walker is dead. You found these pictures and you printed them, so I suppose I should ask you for your permission to publish these." He talked while turning the dog's floppy ears inside out.

I looked at my grandmother, at my mother, then at him. I figured he might not really need my permission. Maybe he was just being polite. Who knew for sure? But I thought of my father then, when he told me I'd know when it was time to do the right thing. Nodding, then whispering my okay, I signed the sheet of paper called "Permission." We drank iced tea, and outside we watched the light go from yellow to slate blue. It was way past that time of day when everyone and everything has gone on home. And this is what we finally did.

On our way back, my grandmother slowed and stopped for three college-age boys standing by the side of the road, next to their station wagon. Their car needed a jump-start, and my grandmother always kept cables and plugs in her trunk. While my mother and the boys hooked up the cables between the two cars, they told us they had come all the way down from New York and were headed for Philadelphia, Mississippi, to help black people register to vote. These boys were white boys, and my grandmother told them that Philadelphia was a strange, backwoodsy sort of town. The one dark-haired, dark-eyed boy told her he knew that and that was why they were staying in Meridian.

It didn't take long for my grandmother's Dinah Shore Chevy to jump-start their station wagon, and after we said goodbye we headed our separate ways. It was late, and we all of us had a long drive ahead.

CHAPTER 17

THAT WEEK WAS OUR SPRING FIELD TRIP, and our class went to the Petrified Forest. I was dreading the day, but then when we all piled out of the school bus, I couldn't help but look down every now and then, secretly hoping to find my pearl earrings.

Our guide showed us arrowheads people had found there. We passed them around. We touched them and held them in the palm of our hand. Mary Alice was wearing a leotard under her skirt, and she was doing something she called pliés, going down-up-up, down-up-up. I wanted her to quit while our guide was talking. I moved away so I could listen more closely to our guide telling us what all and who all had come here before us.

Something changes when you find out about who lived in a place before you, when you find evidence of everyday life from another time in your own time. Those arrowheads came to us as a sort of message, making me feel different about the ground I walked over that day.

My grandmother made a roast that night for dinner, and she showed us her friend's newspaper. There in two full pages were Perry's pictures of his own brutal beating.

"They ran a double truck," my grandmother said.

My mother and I both stared at her.

"A double truck!" she said again, as if she couldn't believe we didn't know what that meant. "That's newspaper talk for two full pages. I've learned a thing or two from my friends through the years."

Our smiling felt strange, but then we grew quiet, looking at the awful truth those pictures revealed.

Somehow everyone at school assumed that I had something to do with the pictures in the paper that now made the national news. My mother and I had heard that Mr. McLemore had been held at the police station, then released with Stone soon after that night we left him there. But after the pictures showed up on the national news, Mr. McLemore and two other men were arrested again, and this time charged with abduction and battery. The police found the black man they had arrested to be innocent and released him.

Stone quit coming to school for a while. In all, he missed something like three weeks. Mary Alice kept coming, though. We heard that Mr. McLemore's business suffered from the publicity, and that Mrs. McLemore wouldn't leave the house. When Stone finally did come back, he came to my locker, and his right eye was black and blue and swollen. I didn't ask what happened, and I could tell Stone appreciated my not asking.

I had thought about this time, when we would finally talk again. For days, I'd dreamed I yelled at Stone, telling him that Perry Walker's blood was on his hands, then in the same dream we were kissing on a bed of pine needles in the Petrified Forest. I woke up feeling embarrassed and guilty.

But he didn't say anything, and his face didn't look angry. We were both so oddly calm in a way I never would have expected. We walked together out of the building. It was raining. The weather had turned balmy. We stood and looked out at the playground near the church and the sidewalks flooding with rainwater.

He told me there would be a trial, and most likely he was going to be used as a witness against his own father. He sounded tired. He looked at me with his handsome dark eyes. "You know, I wasn't sure until I saw the pictures." He stopped himself. "I just wanted you to know I didn't mean for things to happen the way they did." He looked at the ground. It was as if he went back to being a little boy then. "I do what I'm told, but not everything. I tried to stop them, Samantha, but there were so many of them. And it was just me. I didn't go. I wasn't there when they did what they did to Perry in those woods, but then, when I saw those pictures . . ." His eyes filled with tears. "I didn't know they'd taken him there to the Petrified Forest. I wouldn't have taken you there that day, if I'd known. Really, I wouldn't have. But when you found Perry's camera that day, that's when I started to wonder. That's when I started putting two and two together. I guess I was trying to fool myself."

"I'm sorry." It was all I could think of to say.

He shrugged, looked down, and shook his head. "He did wrong, but I had to do right. The police had to see those pictures. Facts don't lie. But he's still my dad." He sighed and put his hand to his eye. "He'll always be my dad."

I put my arm around Stone. He pulled me to him and hugged me close, and for a while, I didn't think either one of us would ever let go. Quietly and in his own way, Stone had done the right thing, after all. We both had, separately. I couldn't help but wonder what we might have accomplished together. In a camera, the aperture is an opening through which light passes. Without the aperture, without this opening, you would never get a picture or any of the masterful photographs I'd learned to appreciate. It had been risky, but Stone and I both opened up a part of our selves to each other. Surely he and I captured something—a moment, a feeling, a document of the heart, to keep, review, and hold close.

When we finally did let go, we looked out toward the street, and I started walking. I needed to get home.

"Watch the puddles," Stone said after me. I turned and nodded, then waved goodbye. The sun coming out lit up the top branches of the pine trees. I wished then that I had my camera. The picture I really wanted? That's the one I never took—a profile of Stone looking skyward, thinking on all those stars. You'd see his nose, his upper Elvis lip, and the silhouette of his eyelashes. That picture would show the Stone I knew and that time when we had only our lives and the heavens to consider, nothing else.

I'd fallen for a boy who liked to sit and watch the sky. He knew about Copernicus, Galileo, Kepler, and Isaac Newton. Maybe what I had with Stone wasn't love. Maybe I just wanted to feel him with me and I wanted him and me both to whisper things like *true love* in each other's ears. Maybe I didn't even care what he whispered so long as he just whispered. He had been more than a friend, and it was the first time I knew what more-than-a-friend meant.

Later I would think about that time I spoke with Stone at

the school, and I would reassure myself. When you're developing pictures, you catch things you hadn't noticed the first time around. Perry explained that to me once. What the mind rejects as ugly it later perceives as beautiful once the underlying patterns have been recognized. Stone wasn't a monster. He was just a boy, and maybe that was the saddest part.

CHAPTER 18

TENSION WAS BUILDING AT MY MOTHER'S COLLEGE, and the faculty took another vote to integrate the college, but administrators feared violence and a loss of white students and money. They formally closed all events to black people and continued to discourage any faculty from teaching, speaking, or even visiting Tougaloo. Even our own teacher, Miss Jenkins at Jackson High School, warned us ninth-graders to steer clear of what she called questionable gatherings in and around the college.

After wearing all the dark mourning clothes, and after weeks of a heartbreakingly beautiful spring, my mother said she was taking me to a reading at her college given by a famous author who she said was "alive and still living among us."

On the evening of the reading, the college was lit up like a monument, as though something historical were about to happen, when in fact it was just a tiny old lady named Eudora Welty coming out to read us a story.

She came and so did the people, from all around, even some students from other colleges and high schools. The day before, the dean reminded everyone of the college's policy, making the event "off-limits" to black people. But they lined up outside anyway.

When it was time for Miss Welty to begin, she waited onstage. We watched as she had a brief exchange with the dean. They were both smiling politely. The dean shook her head no. Miss Welty nodded yes. Then Miss Welty shook her head no and the dean nodded yes. Some of us laughed at the sight.

But then something happened. The doors opened and all the black people waiting outside, the ones the dean wasn't going to let in, came in. Some sat in the front, some in the back, others sat beside us. They sat wherever there was a seat. The auditorium was full up now, dotted with different-colored people. From onstage, we must have been a sight. The corners of Miss Welty's eyes crinkled like tissue paper as she smiled and welcomed us all. She wasn't pretty, but when she smiled and talked and looked at us that way, she was beautiful and we all fell in love with her.

She dedicated the reading to her photographer friend Perry Walker. She told us all she'd met him at the Jitney, and that later he'd contacted her about coming to the college to read. I saw tears well up in my mother's eyes.

She read a story called "Powerhouse" about a Fats Waller concert, which she had written some twenty years before. Listening to her read, we were all together, not listening to a story, but in a music hall called the World Café, listening to jazz and to those musicians talking. When she finished we were all quiet, as though we needed to catch our breath, the drums and saxophones and piano still playing in our minds.

Then she talked about the power of imagination to unite us readers with writers. She said a shared act of imagination could bridge the separateness people feel, even if only for a moment. She talked about our being there, as if us listening to her story meant something important. As if just sitting there together was doing something.

We stood and clapped for her, hundreds of us clapping. Even after she left the stage, we applauded for a long time. We all had that close-together, huddled feeling of being under the same umbrella in the rain. I wanted to sit back down in my seat and replay the story in my head. I just wanted to sit and think.

Afterward, we saw her at a reception in an adjoining room, talking with students who were waiting to shake hands and thank her for coming. My mother had thought to bring my camera, and she gave it to me then. I brought it to my right eye, and then brought it back down again. I hadn't snapped a picture since Perry was still alive. Miss Welty nodded for me to go on, take the picture. She was giving me the go-ahead, so I did. I took a picture of her smiling. I took another of her signing books, and another of her hugging a group, their different-colored arms all wrapped around one another.

My mother took my hand and led me toward the edge of the small crowd. She spoke with Miss Welty. My mother was used to that sort of thing. She could talk to anyone. I saw that now.

"This is my daughter. She takes pictures." My mother sounded proud. "Perry taught her."

Miss Welty looked at me and then offered her hand. It was warm and bony, like my grandmother's. She told me she took pictures once too. She said that was when she learned how to really look at things. Sometimes what you see is more than you want to know. She talked the way Perry used to talk when he talked about photography.

My mother took the camera.

"Let me take a picture of you two," she said.

Miss Welty and I stood side by side, this lady writer and me, her arm around me. I didn't say a word. My mother snapped the picture. I knew by the way she was holding the camera, the picture would be out of focus, but that was okay. I would have it to keep.

That night at home my mother turned my pillow so I could lay my head down on the cool side. We had the house back to ourselves now because my grandmother had left.

"Pookie-poo," she said.

"Moo." For some reason, we spoke in whispers then.

"I'm very proud of you, Samantha," she said. She hardly ever called me Samantha. "You've shown so much courage all through this year."

"I didn't think about being courageous."

"You don't have to think about being courageous to have courage," she said. "I doubt that you even have to *feel* courageous either. Your father wrote me something like that in a letter when he was overseas. You are so much like him."

"You never said that before."

"I'm not sure I thought it before."

I thought about courage and how it must be more hidden than anything like love or hate, grief or mourning. Something inside tells you what's right and you know you have to do that right thing to go on living with yourself and with others.

"It's not like I went to war or into a battle or anything. Not like he did."

"No. It's been *a lot* like fighting in a war. Every day."

When things come clear, when you see it all before you in black and white and you know what's right and what's wrong, what kind of person would stand aside and do nothing? That wouldn't be a person at all, or the human being that Perry said he was—and in fact had been. That would be nothing more than an insect, but at least insects serve a purpose. There comes a time. There just comes a time.

"I miss Dad," I said. "I miss him so much."

"I know," my mother said. "So do I."

Shortly after that evening with Miss Welty, my mother heard from the dean. She didn't get her promotion. My mother didn't get tenure or promoted to associate professor. What that meant was that she had no future at the college. What that meant was that she had to find another job. What that meant was that she most likely had been blacklisted. What that meant was that we might have to move from Jackson and even maybe Mississippi.

When you know you're not wanted, you leave, right? It's as simple as that. Why stay in a place where people hate you daily, or where at least you know no one wants you around? Why stay when it's too dangerous to live out your life? Just because it's home and you've settled? Perry had stayed and he died. Would the black people of Mississippi all begin to disappear the way most of the Choctaw had? Would we?

CHAPTER 19

IT WAS SPRING, not just here but even in the northern states. Neither the Russians that the McLemores and others had anticipated and built their bomb shelter for nor people from outer space had come after all, but the Freedom Riders had, and word was they would be coming again the following year and the year after that and they would keep coming.

My mother's hair had grown, and she brushed the ends to curl *under*, not *out* the way the other mothers wore their hair. It was different and I liked it on her. She wore bright-colored dresses with bold patterns she said looked like Mondrian paintings. "When I stand and walk forward, you get the full effect," she liked to say when people commented.

A copy of Perry's book of photographs came in the mail, and together my mother and I looked through it, sometimes even preferring the thin sheet of tissue covering the more violent and disturbing photographs in the book—the images muted that way and fuzzy, covered with the tissue. There was an introduction written by an editor of *Life*, quoting what Perry had once said to him. "Life is what it is at any second. A snapshot. Nothing more."

"Did he really believe that?" I asked my mother.

She shrugged and smiled.

He had shown me how a picture was balanced, how what needed to be seen was what should be focused. It felt strange sitting there looking through all these terrible, good pictures. They were beautiful pictures of horrible things. How could beauty come from such ugliness? It didn't seem right or good, but maybe close to some kind of truth.

I grew my bangs out and parted my hair down the middle, more the way my mother's college coeds wore their hair and not the way Mary Alice wore hers. For the first time, I actually fit into my bra. I wore knee socks now instead of bobby socks, but my mother still wouldn't allow me to wear hose, let alone the green fishnet stockings or go-go boots Mary Alice and her friends wore.

Mary Alice had written to Glenn Campbell and John Wayne, and neither had written back. She took up the baton because she said twirlers always won the beauty pageants. Even though Mary Alice told everyone that her brother Stone had been "disowned," she also said he had dumped me, and because I was so "marked," surely nobody would ever go out with me ever again. "If I don't marry," Mary Alice said loudly one day in the cafeteria, "I might as well be dead." Mr. McLemore was out on bail and facing a prison sentence. He stayed in his house mostly. Rumors circulated about Stone. Someone said he thought he saw Stone hitching a ride toward Alabama. Someone else thought she saw him at the grocery store. He became like a ghost.

Word got out that my mother and I were probably leaving, so at that moment in time no one bothered us. As we ended our year at school studying balanced proportions and Fibonacci numbers in Miss Jenkins's math class, we hunted for a pattern in the senseless and unpatterned acts occurring nightly in Jackson. With order came understanding and beauty in our mathematical formulas. Chaos and a lack of pattern were ugly . . . or were they? That same spring, my mother was giving lectures about modern art, showing slides of crazy-looking drip paintings by a man named Jackson Pollock, whom some called Action Jackson.

For our final communications project, Miss Jenkins asked us each to report on an "outside event." It could be either local or national, but it had to take place outside our school walls. She said the administration wanted us to be "more aware." Miss Jenkins didn't seem to be too happy about that.

Mary Alice talked about attending the Mississippi State Fair the previous summer with her family. Miss Jenkins actually clapped at the end of Mary Alice's presentation. Others reported on church events and family reunions. Ears, whom I called Tempe now, talked about the stickball games he played when he and other members of the Choctaw nation got together. He brought in his game equipment and demonstrated, barefoot, for the class. Everybody, even Miss Jenkins, liked his report.

I borrowed an easel from Perry's things and I propped up pictures one after the other, pausing between each picture to give everyone an eyeful. I showed the pictures I took at the lunch counter at the drugstore, the ones Perry had helped me develop. I showed all of them, ending with the picture of the waitress staring at Willa Mae, the picture I called "Hate." Then I showed the pictures I took of the woman writer, Miss Welty. I showed her smiling and signing her books. I showed pictures of her hugging people, both black and white. I didn't say much during my presentation. I wasn't much interested in speechmaking anymore. Besides, you know what they say about pictures, right? They tell a thousand words. So why make it a thousand and one?

I knew Miss Jenkins wouldn't like my presentation even though I showed not one but two outside events. By then I didn't care about her or Mary Alice or my grades. I did care what Tempe thought, so I looked at just him while I stood in front of the class and ran through all the pictures. Soon we would all go our separate ways. Families would move across the state, some even out of state. Jackson and a good part of Mississippi had proven to be a difficult place to live. Tempe and his family would move to Philadelphia, Mississippi, where his mother had family and his father hoped to find work. Miss Jenkins would surprise both Tempe and me by sending in his cicada report to Mississippi State in Starkville, where he received a camp scholarship to study science over the summer.

"Pictures are a form of communication," I said at the very end of my presentation. "When we communicate we have a bill of rights that guarantees us freedom of speech and expression." I looked around at all the faces in my class. I waited for someone, anyone, to just nod. "Right?" I said. Tempe blinked. The others looked blank. Someone yawned.

My mother sent out job applications, and in May she got word about a well-paying job as an assistant professor at a university in Boston. She got refitted with a new hearing aid, one that let in all the sound so she didn't have to keep turning it up or down.

We didn't want to go. My mother and I didn't want to leave Mississippi or the South. We left because we had to.

Together we repainted the house and put it on the market, selling it within a month's time. That summer we planned to rent a place in Boston, then see some of the East Coast and tour Washington, D.C., for the first time, and with the extra money made from selling our house, my mother and I planned the trip she had always wanted. We were going to spend ten days in Greece, walking the steps up to places like the Acropolis and the Parthenon, finding out more about what had once been a nearly perfect civilization and democracy.

It was going to be a new start. Because we were moving so far away, my aunt said it would be too inconvenient for her to send my cousin Tine's old clothes, which meant that I would have to find my own clothes, a hunt I both dreaded and anticipated.

We began packing, and at the end of every day, our little house was filled with more brown boxes that held our dishes, linens, books. One afternoon I opened the kitchen pantry and stared at what we had left of my grandmother's fruits and vegetables in their glass jars—the garlic and dill bobbing like the snow in those wintry Christmas paperweights I admired in storefront windows. I understood then why Perry had taken a picture of the jars.

At night I looked out my window at the moon growing fuller over the roof of the house across the street.

It was hardest to say goodbye to Willa Mae. She told me I was responsible for knowing where she packed the vacuum cleaner bags and that I had to do a better job of helping out more around the house, because now it was just going to be my mother and me. No Willa Mae helping. No Grandmother coming during emergencies. I was scared of leaving, of moving away from what I knew to something I did not know at all. I remembered Willa Mae telling me her biggest fear: that she would do something she'd regret. She'd told me fear was just one more thing you could change into something else, something else like anger or even love.

I wrapped up the picture of Willa Mae laughing and gave it to her. When she opened it in front of me, she smiled.

"I *will* miss you," she said, sitting down with me on a box to eat our last meal together—peanut butter and jelly sandwiches. She told me sometimes bad things happened for a good reason. If my mother had gotten her promotion, we wouldn't be headed for Boston. Either way you looked at it, we wouldn't have had much of a second chance at starting over if we stayed.

"Oh, Willa Mae." I was so sad, I could barely hold my head up.

"You can call me Bill, " she said. Only those close to Willa Mae were allowed to call her Bill. "So? How you do?"

"Not too good," I said.

I was going to miss tending my grandmother's kitchen garden with Tine every summer, cooking and canning our harvests. I didn't know what was ahead of us. All I knew was what and whom we were leaving behind. I knew these streets, the houses, which trees were the best trees to climb, which hills were the best to skate down. I knew this place. And I could not see my way into knowing any other place as well as I knew Mississippi.

Willa Mae put down her sandwich and moved closer. She drew me to her, keeping her arm around me. I couldn't remember when I was ever this close to Willa Mae. She smelled of tobacco and ginger both. "In Mississippi, people have a way of holding on to the past," she said. "The mud here is sticky. But sometimes you got to let go."

On our last day, the day we were ready to pull out, I checked under the hood of our car before we left. I'd gotten into the habit after I'd read about how bombs were planted there under the hoods of cars during the night.

My mother and I got in. She backed out the drive. We waved to our house. We did all the things a body does to say goodbye. But even as we drove away from our house I missed it, missed the camellias that grew as big as trees, the monkey grass, the pines, the summer heat. But at the same time, I felt such a relief.

My mother sat in the driver's seat, smiling. We would go up north and something else new would begin. She knew this and I knew this. Our knowledge was behind her smile.

I wanted to be mad at everyone in the South who had done so much wrong. I was ready to be mad at the whole state of Mississippi, but then out of nowhere I looked at the road, then up at the sky, and thought, *Thank you.* Without all the bad, I wouldn't recognize the good. I wouldn't know. I wouldn't know about feeling bad for people and maybe I wouldn't know so much about feeling good for people either. I knew more, and this felt like a new old coat from my grandmother. I needed it all to feel this way, and I wondered what it might be if a whole country felt the same.

Already heat mirages rose from the asphalt highway as we drove. Lines of pine trees stood as still and straight as soldiers on either side of the road.

I had my camera and the jar full of cicada shells I'd collected the summer before, the summer we'd moved to Mississippi. The summer before. That was the way I would always think of that time. The summer before I learned about love and hate all in the same year. The summer before it all happened.

When my mother and I left Mississippi, we were just a month away from what was later called Freedom Summer, when all the real anger broke out. In June of 1963, a man named Medgar Evers was shot dead in his garage, a man with a house in Jackson just like ours, a man with a wife and children, a man with a carport, monkey grass, and a nice lawn. All of it, like ours. Except that he was dead and we were not, because he was black and we were not, and he had stayed.

In the car leaving Jackson with my mother, I looked at the empty shells through the glass, shaking them a little. They came up from out of the ground making all that noise, seemingly out of nowhere, when in fact they'd been there all along, there among us all along. They came up, baring themselves to the world, screeching, singing, humming, whistling, then they disappeared, marking the trees with their own remains. I thought about the nonstop hum my mother and I both always thought we heard all that year, even after the cicadas had died away. Maybe it was the land itself warning us, pleading with us: *Do something.*

My mother learned how to control the volume level of outside voices and other everyday disturbances by artificial means. She simply turned off her hearing aid. But I still hear the voices of Tempe and Willa Mae and Stone and Mary

Alice, Aunt Ida, my cousin Tine, Miss Jenkins, Perry, and my grandmother. When I care to listen, I hear their voices humming inside my head, and every seven years, when the cicadas come out, I hear them all clearly talking and shouting, all of them all over again. They click and buzz from the ground and from the trunks of the trees. Their shells are scattered everywhere. Their voices are a reminder. *Don't forget,* they are saying. *Don't you dare forget.*

Years later, after school and several odd summer jobs, I would take newspaper positions in Cincinnati, Tallahassee, Atlanta, and then finally in Chicago, where I stayed on, photographing the news of the day. I tell colleagues about the past as I knew it. I show them pictures I took back then, pictures that look similar to some of the news pictures I take now.

"Mom, you know what?" I said in the car.

"What."

"I love you and I like you. Both."

She kept her eyes on the road, and her hands on the wheel of her beige VW Bug with the rusty fenders, but I saw the right side of her face break into a smile. Sunlight lit her up. Perry Walker once told me to find the shadows first in order to recognize my light source. I lifted the camera to my eye and focused.

AUTHOR'S NOTE

January 2010

Sources of Light is a mix of fact and fiction. I lived in Jackson, Mississippi, with my parents and sister from 1963 to 1969. We didn't experience and witness everything that Samantha does, but we did have neighbors who were threatened or beaten, and my mother had a close friend who was murdered. I never attended a Jackson High School, and Eudora Welty never dedicated a reading to the fictional Perry Walker, though she did give a memorable reading of "Powerhouse" to an integrated audience at Millsaps College, where my mother taught and participated with her in a panel discussion. My sister and I used to play in the woods behind Miss Welty's house in Jackson, and my sister claims she once saved me from drowning in a little creek there.

We all at one time brush up against history or historical figures that have an impact on our lives. My parents attended a Joan Baez concert in Jackson one year, and afterward a young man from out of state couldn't start his station wagon. My father offered to jump-start it. He and the young man spoke briefly and the two went on their way. The following year my father recognized both the station wagon and the young man in the newspapers. The young man my father recognized was Michael Schwerner, one of the four civil rights workers murdered in Philadelphia, Mississippi. The FBI found the burned-out station wagon before they found the bodies.

For a long time I was ashamed to say I was from Mississippi. I even told some of the jokes most people know by now. Question: What's got four *i*'s and can't see? Answer: Mississippi.

When people asked where I was from, sometimes I just said "the South," or "north of New Orleans." After all, how could this one state produce magnolias, pine forests, Eudora Welty, William Faulkner, Richard Wright, *and* the Citizens' Council? How was that possible? How could I love a state that did such horrors to its own? Now I'm beginning to understand.

Writers thrive on conflict—hopefully in our work and not in our lives. Our job is to reflect and interpret trouble. After a time, we should become skilled at finding the shadows so that perhaps our readers may recognize the light.

James Meredith graduated from the University of Mississippi in August 1963 with the help of 500 U.S. marshals' nearly constant security. He was the first black person ever to do so. In late August that same year, Martin Luther King Jr. delivered a speech called "I Have a Dream" to 200,000 people in Washington, D.C.

But for a long time hate poisoned everything, especially in the South.

In September of 1963 a bomb exploded during a Sunday school class at the 16th Street Baptist Church in Birmingham, Alabama, killing four children. They identified one of the victims by her shoes. Then in November, just days before Thanksgiving, President Kennedy was assassinated. Five years later, Martin Luther King Jr. was shot dead in Memphis, and a month after that the president's brother Robert Kennedy was killed in Los Angeles.

The Vietnam War, which started in a country no one had heard of, lasted sixteen years, ending only a few years after another battle called Watergate. In 1974 India joined other nations to explode a nuclear device, and the world couldn't help but look with wonder at pictures of the surface of Mars, and later even of Jupiter.

Sometimes when I tell my son about growing up in Missis-sippi I sound like my older relatives when they used to talk about the Civil War years and the hard times that followed. My 1960s are like their 1860s, for in my lifetime, people in the United States went out and beat and killed other people and more often than not got away with it, got away with murder. Still, I think it's important to talk about such things in order to know. You can't pick and choose your history, and you can't turn away from it either.

Many people tried to talk me out of writing about the 1960s in Mississippi. "That's all in the past," several southern friends told me. "We've moved on, so you should too." But I think it's important to look back and reflect on the past, even if it's only to see how far we've come.

And now? Now the forty-fourth president of the United States is Barack Obama, a man of color, powerful proof that we really are capable of judging people by the content of their character and not by the color of their skin. This hardly seemed possible. That difficult, violent time in Mississippi wasn't so long ago. But America is a different America now. The South is a different South. I know because my husband, my son, and I spend a lot of time on the Gulf Coast of Mississippi with my parents in a town that has survived two of the world's biggest hurricanes. We are all survivors—the people of this country, the South, this town, my parents, my sister, and me—and we all keep coming back.

ACKNOWLEDGMENTS

I'd like to thank professors Dale Edwards and Cris Hoshwender at the University of Evansville and Richard Brown at Mississippi State for their help with endomology and cicadas. I'd also like to thank Suzanne Marrs, Millsaps College, and the Eudora Welty Foundation, the John F. Kennedy Library, Gary and Cindy Bayer and the Writers' Gathering Jerusalem, Alan Huffman and Scott Saalman for their recollections, the Ya-Yas, the Bibliochicks and the Inkling Book groups for their discussions, and the Social Literary Circle for their food recipes from the 1960s. And always, my thanks go to my agent, Jennie Dunham, and to Margaret Raymo, Karen Walsh, Nadya Guerrero-Pezzano, and the many other talented people at Houghton Mifflin Harcourt.